MURDER AT OCEAN VIEW COLLEGE

Karen Batchelor

City College of San Francisco

Houghton Mifflin Company
Boston   New York

Custom Publishing Editor: Mary McGibbons
Custom Publishing Production Manager: Tina Kozik
Custom Publishing Project Coordinator: Anisha Palmer

Cover Designer: Beth Fountain

Printed in the United States of America.

ISBN-13: 978-0-618-76947-6
ISBN-10: 0-618-76947-1
N-06314

2 3 4 5 6 7 8 9 – CCI – 08 07 06

 **Houghton Mifflin**
                    Custom Publishing

222 Berkeley Street • Boston, MA 02116

Address all correspondence and order information to the above address.

ACKNOWLEDGEMENTS

I am indebted to a number of people for helping this book appear on bookshelves and in classrooms:

To Charlie Hoenesh, Chair of the Administration of Justice Department at City College of San Francisco for generously sharing information about that program.

To Randi Slaughter, Earl Hayes, and John Ventura for classroom testing.

To Donna Champion, Lynn Millar, Jeannette Taylor, Ana Manwaring, Shelley Singer, and Kate Farrell for reading, editing and commenting on the manuscript.

To Claire Drucker for encouragement in the very beginning.

To my writing group for listening so patiently for what seemed like years.

To my students who have suffered through several drafts, and who have enthusiastically asked again and again when this book would be finished and where they could buy it.

Thank you one and all.

Contents

Chapter One

Discovery

AT 7:30 A.M., the elevator was out again, so Danny Soto, student cop, took the steps two at a time to the seventh floor faculty offices. He held a cell phone in one hand and in the other his police baton. On the seventh floor landing, he darted down the short hallway toward the heavy outer office door and pulled it open. He hurried inside.

Jade was standing still, as if frozen, outside Ms. Quinn's wide-open office door. She turned her head mechanically as Danny approached. She must have lost her cap sometime this morning because her long, black hair hung down her back and over her shoulders. He saw that her eyes were glazed over from shock and the knuckles on her left hand were white where she held the phone in a death grip. On the floor around her feet were several sheets of white paper with her boot prints on them.

"Are you OK?" he asked, placing his large hand on her shoulder and automatically pushing her hair back from her forehead. He looked at her face—smooth skin, features that reminded him of her Chinese heritage.

"Yes." Jade answered in a tiny whisper. She shook her head as if to shake loose cobwebs, and then cleared her throat. "I'm OK, Danny. You have to. . ." she hesitated. "You have to look. She's in there." She pointed at the open office door.

Danny turned and stepped briskly to the door. His eyes fell on a shiny blue high-heeled shoe alone in the middle of the floor.

"She's over there," Jade's voice, stronger and louder now, came from right behind him. She touched his arm and pointed at the wooden filing cabinet to the right of the far wall. There she was. Ms. Quinn was stuffed between the tall, overloaded bookcase and the heavy oak filing cabinet.

Danny stepped closer. Jade stepped up beside him. Ms. Quinn looked like she was almost standing up. Her legs were bent slightly at the knee and she was uneven because she was missing the shoe on her right foot. Her head sagged onto her chest and her long blonde hair covered her face. Her shoulders were squeezed into the tight space. She wore a blue wool dress and her pale hands hung down in front of her. Her fingernails were painted blood red and she was still wearing the diamond engagement ring that everyone had been talking about for the last two weeks. There was no doubt about it. Ms. Ruby Quinn was dead.

Danny caught his breath. Jade took his hand. They leaned against the bookcase for support. He put his hand on the filing cabinet and leaned closer to the body, trying to discover the cause of death.

Jade jerked his arm. "Danny! Don't mess with a crime scene."

"Oh, right," and he moved away again.

Breathing heavily, they moved together out of Ms. Quinn's office and over to the study carrel on the opposite wall. Danny offered a chair to Jade. He stood.

"Did you call the captain?" Danny asked.

"I tried. He wasn't in yet. I called you because…" she hesitated. "Because they taught us that you're always supposed to call your partner."

Danny nodded. "We still have to call Captain Mitchell. But tell me. Tell me about it." Danny tried to sound like he was used to finding dead bodies on campus every morning.

Jade took a deep breath before she could speak. She started slowly. Then the words came rolling out, fast and smooth. "I found her like this. I had an appointment with her this morning at 7:00. She said she always got here early. I should just come on in. Bring my paper." She hesitated. "So I did." She just then remembered her paper. She stood and started picking up the pages from the floor.

Danny started to pace back and forth. He was a pacer. Pacing helped him think better.

"Was the outer door unlocked?" It's supposed to be locked before 8:00."

"It was open. I just walked right in."

"Was her office door open?" he asked.

"Just a little. I knocked and called her name. When nobody answered, I opened the door all the way, And I saw her. You know, like that. Like, dead." She sat down again and put her paper on the study desk.

"Oh, my God, Danny! Who would want to kill Ms. Quinn? Everybody liked her. I thought so anyway. Who would do this? Oh, God, Danny, I'll be a suspect, won't I?" She covered her face with her hands.

Danny put his arm around her and tried to comfort her. "Of

course, they'll have to question you, but I'm sure that no one will really suspect you. How could you murder anybody?" He smiled at her.

Jade finally lifted her head. "We have to call Captain Mitchell. He'll make the report to the Ocean View City cops."

"Come on, Jade, this is our first murder case. Let's not screw it up." Danny was getting excited.

"This cannot be our first murder case. Are you forgetting? We're just campus cops. In training. We haven't even graduated from Ocean View College. We haven't even been accepted at the police academy yet. We're not actually cops yet. If we try to get involved here, we're only asking for trouble. For sure."

Danny frowned. He knew she was right. "Yes. I know. We can direct traffic, write tickets and respond to an emergency. That's it. That's all."

Jade stood and touched his cheek. "Danny, maybe they'll ask us to help. I'll call the captain."

She took the cell phone from her pocket and called the campus police chief. She could hear a little yawn as Captain Charlie Mitchell picked up on the second ring.

"Ocean View College. Police Department. Captain Mitchell speaking."

Jade took a deep breath. "This is student officer Jade Lee. Officer Soto and I would like to speak to you." She handed the phone to Danny, but he pointed at her.

"You talk to him. You found her."

She froze again for just a minute, then placed the cell phone to her ear.

"Captain Mitchell, there appears to be a homicide victim on the seventh floor of Peterson Hall. Ms. Quinn. English teacher. Officer Soto and I are at the scene waiting for your instructions."

Jade paused, in control now. "Yes, sir." She turned off the cell phone and turned to Danny. "Charlie is on his way."

Chapter Two

Captain Mitchell Investigates

WHILE DANNY and Jade were discussing the possibility of a murderer loose on campus, Captain Mitchell dashed in. They turned their heads at the same time to look up at him. They watched him take off his cap and scrape his thick fingers over his shiny, bald head.

"Danny, Jade," he nodded at the two student cops.

"Captain Mitchell," Danny said, "she's in there." He pointed to the open office door.

The captain turned his eyes in that direction and three pairs of eyes focused on the blue high-heeled shoe in the middle of the floor. Captain Mitchell stepped inside. The students looked at each other, shrugged and followed him.

"Don't touch anything," Captain Mitchell growled. "This is a crime scene."

"Yes, sir," they said at the same time. They stood still and tried not to breathe too loudly. They followed the captain with their eyes, afraid to get too close. This was, they knew, an opportunity to see an investigation first hand. Looking at his back, they could see him stiffen when he saw the body. He walked closer. He shook his head. From his hip pocket, he pulled out a pair of thin plastic gloves and put them on. He looked at the teacher's body for a minute before he pushed the hair up from her face and studied it.

"It's Ruby," he said in a low voice.

Then, he cleared his throat and started talking as if to a class of students.

"There are no unusual marks on the head or neck area. Blood on the dress. Looks like a stab wound. It's round. Very small. Not a knife. More like an ice pick, or maybe a pencil."

Jade and Danny were wide-eyed. They looked at each other and whispered, "Pencil?"

Captain Mitchell picked up the limp wrist and felt for a pulse. "No pulse. She's dead. " He turned to Danny and Jade.

"Somebody stabbed her. In the heart."

Their eyes grew wider and Jade clutched her hand over her own heart as if she felt the pain of the stab.

Captain Mitchell turned away from the body to face the students. His eyes scanned the room quickly. Jade and Danny's eyes followed. They watched him pull a little notepad from his pocket and scribble some notes. Then he moved his eyes slowly around the room.

The body was stuffed tightly between a heavy bookcase and a filing cabinet on the north wall of the office. The top drawer of the filing cabinet was open part way. The drawer was filled with manila folders, each one labeled, and a stack of papers with rubber bands around it. On the top of the pile, there was a blue slip stamped with the date and "Duplicating Services."

The five shelves of the bookcase were all filled. The books were arranged by topic and size. Nothing seemed to be out of place. The bookcase was against the wall and formed a corner with the windows. The windows looked outside onto the new football field.

Danny stepped to the window and looked out. There was a ledge all around the building on each floor. The ledge was about twelve inches wide. He was looking at the pigeons sitting there when the captain's voice brought him back to attention.

"Don't touch anything," Captain Mitchell barked.

"Just looking out the window. Didn't touch anything," Danny replied and raised his hands palms up to show they were empty. The captain did not comment but continued his investigation of Ms. Quinn's office.

In front of the window was a small desk holding a computer and beside it, a chair on rollers. The computer was on and there was a screen saver with several very colorful fish swimming back and forth across the computer screen. On the south wall, there were three coat hooks. One held a blue raincoat, and a blue umbrella hung from another one. The third hook was empty.

Captain Mitchell looked thoughtfully at every inch of Ms. Quinn's office. Danny and Jade watched but did not speak. When he was finished examining the office, Captain Mitchell turned around and scratched his scalp again.

"Now," he addressed Danny and Jade. "What were you two doing here?"

"I had, uh, I had an appointment with, with Ms. Quinn." Jade stammered then cleared her throat.

"And you?" he pointed at Danny.

"Jade called me."

"I'm the captain. You're supposed to call me."

"You weren't in, sir. So she called me."

"Officer Lee. You the one who found her?" the captain barked again.

"I did," Jade looked straight at him.

"Like this?"

"Yes, sir."

They felt the captain's sharp eyes moving from one to the other and back. Then he spoke again. "City police are on the way. You two are going to have to go downtown and answer some questions." He scratched his bald head again and started to walk away. He turned back toward Danny and Jade. "Well, come on. Let's go."

Jade grabbed Danny's hand and they followed the captain out the door.

Coming toward them as they left was another officer carrying yellow tape to place across Ms. Quinn's office door.

Chapter Three

Crystal Rides Along

GRIPPING DANNY'S hand tightly, Jade followed him and Captain Mitchell down the six flights of stairs. It seemed like a long time ago that she had entered the building to meet with Ms. Quinn. Jade kept her eyes straight ahead, looking at the captain's back. She wondered what a real police investigation would be like, and she frowned as she realized that she and Danny were the ones who would have to answer the questions this time. Danny turned to look at her. He wasn't smiling and she realized that she wasn't, either.

In Criminal Investigation classes, student police officers had to practice questioning witnesses. Jade had done this, and Danny had, too. But today was the first time she might be a suspected criminal. She tried to calm herself down. Danny squeezed her hand. She imagined that he could read her thoughts. He knew she worried easily. She wondered if he was also worried about the possibility of going to jail. Of course, he had to know she was innocent.

He looked at her again, and she tried to smile.

As the captain opened the main door to the building, a blast of cold air hit them all in the face. Because Ocean View is on the California coast, the weather is often cold and foggy. Jade felt the cold blast and shivered. Danny dropped her hand and put his arm around her. She looked up at him and gave him a weak smile. He hugged her tighter.

Just outside the main door, she caught sight of Crystal Jackson—20 years old, another student police officer, the leader of their unit and Jade's closest friend. Jade looked up at Crystal, who stood just over six feet tall—a full ten inches taller than Jade. Crystal was also black and beautiful. Her smooth skin was the color of coffee with cream. Before deciding to study Criminal Justice at Ocean View College, Crystal had been a model for some department stores in the Los Angeles area. Sometimes Jade could get her to tell stories about the photo shoot locations she went to, about the men she often got involved with, and the nice restaurants and night clubs they liked to take her to. Jade was enchanted with Crystal's former life, and she sometimes wondered why Crystal had decided to make such a big career change. Why did she want to be a police officer anyway? It certainly wasn't glamorous.

Jade and Danny moved up beside Captain Mitchell. Jade's face formed a weak smile when she stopped beside Crystal. It looked like she was waiting for them. Jade thought she should be quiet, so she only nodded her head at Crystal. Jade stood still, close to Danny, and listened as Crystal addressed the captain.

"Good morning, Captain Mitchell. Police secretary told me that there is a situation here. A crime scene. I thought I might be able to help. Anything I can do?" Jade could see just a tiny smile as Crystal turned her head in Jade's direction. Jade began to relax. Good old, dependable Crystal.

"Everything is under control, Officer Jackson." He turned to Danny and Jade, then back to Crystal. "Officers Soto and Lee are going to ride downtown with me. We'll be back later."

"Would you like me to ride along, Captain? I could help you with the report."

Captain Mitchell removed his hat again and scratched his bald head. Everyone knew he hated writing reports. "Well, you are the leader of their unit. Maybe that's not such a bad idea. It will give you a chance to witness a real police questioning."

"Yes, sir. Happy to help out." Crystal reached out and Jade could feel a reassuring hand on her shoulder.

Danny and Jade let out their breath at the same time. Jade was relieved to have Crystal come along and she thought Danny looked relieved, too. He knew how close the two young women were. Danny held Jade's hand and helped her into the back of the campus police car, which was painted on the side with the red and white Ocean View College logo.

Crystal sat in the front with Captain Mitchell. As Jade and Danny settled in the back seat, Jade realized immediately that this was where suspected criminals always sat. She saw Danny start to crack his knuckles. She put her hands over his to stop him. She whispered, "You know that's a disgusting habit, Danny! You only do it when you're nervous."

"Well, you're right about that. I'm nervous. How can we possibly prove that we had nothing to do with Ms. Quinn's murder? And, I'm pretty sure they don't have any other suspects right now."

Jade's eyes darkened in a frown and she fell silent again.

At the city police station, Jade and Danny followed Crystal and Captain Mitchell, who were following a clerk with the city police department. They all went into a small room with a long wooden table. At the head of the table was the Chief of Police for the city of Ocean View. Captain Mitchell took a seat next to the chief and Crystal sat between him and Jade.

The walls of the room were gray without any pictures or posters. The light was dim and the temperature in the room was cool.

The city police chief was a large, older man with a full head of white hair. He looked at the three students with a stone face and nodded toward Captain Mitchell, then spoke to open the meeting. "Now this is an informal interrogation. You are not being charged with any crime. We just want to hear what happened." He looked at Crystal. All eyes turned on Crystal. She smiled and spoke calmly.

"Chief, these two student officers discovered a body on campus at Ocean View College this morning." She waved her hand toward Jade and Danny. "They are the ones who need to tell the story."

Then the chief looked at Danny, indicating that he should speak. Everybody turned and looked at Danny. Then Danny spoke. "Actually, Chief, Jade—Officer Lee—is the one who discovered the body. She should give you the story." He turned his head to smile at Jade. The other three people in the room turned like robots and looked at Jade.

The chief's face was blank. He nodded to Jade, indicating that she should tell what she had seen and heard. She cleared her throat and began talking in a quiet voice, but as she got into the telling of the story, she relaxed and grew more confident. Danny helped when his turn came and Captain Mitchell added what he knew about the crime scene and the story the students had told.

The Chief of Police tape recorded the entire procedure. Then he dismissed them and told Jade and Danny that they were not to take any long trips for a while. They needed to be available for further questioning. Then, he smiled. Jade wished that he had smiled at the beginning of the interview. She would have felt better.

On the ride back to campus, there was silence in the car. Jade was thinking about the murder and wondering who could have done such a horrible thing.

Chapter Four

In Duplicating

THE DUPLICATING room was buzzing with activity. There was a long line of teachers and student helpers waiting to use the photocopy machine. Danny stopped in front of Coach Kelly who was at the end of the line. The coach was carrying his clipboard, as usual, and had stuck his shiny blue pencil through the graying hair above his ear. He was wearing a red jacket with "Coach Kelly" printed on the breast pocket.

"Hi, Coach. Ready for the new season?"

"It's a pretty good team, Danny, but I wish you would change your mind and go out for football this year."

Danny shrugged. "You know I'd love to, but I have to concentrate on my classes. When I play football, my grades suffer. I can't seem to think of anything but football."

Coach Kelly smiled and put his hand on Danny's shoulder.

"Well, if you ever change your mind, let me know."

Danny excused himself and broke through the line to reach the counter. There was Amber Jones. She was smiling brightly up at Danny. He took a quick look at her and saw a familiar face and figure that he usually tried to avoid. He tried to smile.

Amber had broad football shoulders and she was several pounds overweight. Her hair was long and dark and teased high on top of her head. There were three green stripes in her hair running from the front to the back of her head, and there was a little green bow peeking out of the top. She wore very large silver hoop earrings and had a tattoo of a snake wrapped around her wrist. The snake's tongue was long and pointed. Amber's short fingernails were painted dark green, and matched the green paint above her eyes and the extra color in her hair. Her lipstick was the color of an over-ripe avocado.

Danny took a deep breath.

"Hey, Danny. What's up?"

"Hey, Amber. I came to pick up some flyers Captain Mitchell wanted photocopied. Is the order ready?"

Amber turned her head to the side and lowered her lashes.

"Let me check on that," she almost whispered and gave his hand a little pat, making the snake dance on her wrist. She turned away for the order. Danny made a face and wiped his hand where she had touched him. She was the same old Amber who had been chasing him since high school, when he was a wilder type of guy, often on the edge of trouble. Amber didn't seem to understand that he wore a uniform these days—a police officer's uniform.

She returned with a large pile of white paper held together with a rubber band. There was a blue sheet that the duplicating office always put on each order to identify the lot, the person who ordered it, and the person who picked it up. This was for office records.

Amber spoke brightly. "Oh. These are the flyers asking for anyone with information about the murder to speak up. Isn't that kind of dumb? Do you think anyone is actually going to tell the cops anything? I mean, like, even if they knew something?"

"Maybe not," Danny said. "The captain is trying to cover all the bases."

"Speaking of bases, that reminds me. You going to the game, Danny?"

"I'm going to try, but with the murder investigation here on campus, Captain Mitchell is keeping us all pretty busy. Jade and I are both putting in extra hours."

At the mention of Jade's name, Amber's eyes turned cold and she bit her lip. Then she spoke again. "Well, it is the first football game of the season. Everybody's going." She paused, By the way, is there anything new in the investigation? I heard that Mr. Taylor did it. From the Math Department. You know, her boyfriend."

"I haven't heard that. You know, Amber, I can't talk about the case. But, hey, maybe I'll see you at the game."

The smile returned to her face before Danny nodded and turned to leave the room. At the door, he turned back to Amber and said, "By the way, Amber, there are no bases in football. Bases are for baseball."

Amber's smile fell from her lips.

As Danny walked out, he saw Coach Kelly biting his lip to keep from laughing.

Chapter Five

Danny and CJ

DANNY ALMOST RAN out of the duplicating room on his way to Captain Mitchell's office. The captain was waiting for these flyers and he had told Danny to hurry. He sped around a corner and hit a tall person very hard. It was Crystal. The pile of flyers fell out of his arms and scattered all over the first floor hallway. He threw his hands in the air, then looked at Crystal, who looked surprised.

"Gee, Danny. Sorry." She bent down on one knee and started to pick up the mess. Danny bent down, too, and quickly, they began to gather the flyers into one pile.

"Hey, CJ, I should have been more careful. In too big of a hurry, I guess. My mom always told me not to run in the house. Now I see why."

Crystal laughed. "Danny, you are the only one who gets away with calling me 'CJ.' Anybody else would get a fist in the face! Anyway, why are you in such a rush?" She was holding one of the flyers in her hand and looked down at it.

"Hey," she said, "these are the flyers the captain ordered." She looked at it more carefully and read aloud. "The campus police would like to talk with anyone who was on campus early Tuesday morning, September 10. This is in regard to the murder of Ms. Ruby Quinn. If you have any information at all, please come to the police bungalow immediately."

When she finished reading, she looked at Danny again and asked, "Do you think anyone saw anything, and if they did, would they be brave enough to come forward with the information?"

Danny held the papers in his hands and tapped one edge of the pile against the floor, trying to fit them all into a neat and tidy stack. Then he raised himself to a standing position before answering Crystal's question.

"I guess it's worth a try," he said, "the captain is trying to cover all the bases. You never know. Maybe somebody saw something. We need all the pieces of the puzzle before we can figure it out. You know, Amber just asked me that same question. She said nobody's going to say anything even if they did see something. People don't want to get involved."

"Amber? What has she got to do with this?" Crystal asked a little annoyed.

"Nothing, I guess. She was just talking. She said Mr. Taylor did it. I guess that's the gossip around the campus."

"I heard that one, too," Crystal said. "And you know, Danny," she looked right at him now, "Amber has a crush on you."

Danny felt his face get hot, but he smiled and shrugged. "I know. Anyway," he continued, "the captain told me he wanted these flyers ASAP. So I have to run. See you later." He nodded to her and took a big step away before adding, "CJ."

Crystal jumped up and followed him out the door and up the hill. "I'll go with you. I have to see the captain about making a trade on the schedule."

As they walked up the hill together, Danny was aware again that Crystal was about two inches taller than he was. He had to look up just slightly to talk to her. Their long legs moved them quickly up the hill to the little old building where the Criminal Justice Department had its offices and classrooms. This was also head-quarters for the campus police.

After a minute, Crystal spoke again, "Danny, a minute ago you were talking about this murder investigation and said 'we.' Just what do you mean by 'we'? What do you have to do with this investigation?"

Danny turned his eyes toward Crystal. "Since Jade and I are at least on a list of suspects, I think we should be trying to clear our names, don't you? Want to help, CJ?"

"No, I don't. You can actually get in more trouble going against the captain's orders. You could be expelled from the Criminal Justice Department and ruin your chances of getting into the Police Academy. If I were you, Danny, I would leave the investigation to the captain."

"But—"

"I know for a fact," Crystal said, interrupting him, "that Captain Mitchell told you and Jade to stay out of this investigation." Her face looked hard.

"So, CJ, you don't want to help. But, you aren't going to say anything to the captain, are you? You wouldn't! Jade's your best friend! You couldn't report your best friend!"

She looked thoughtful for a second, then said, "OK. Let's make a deal. I won't say anything to the captain about your investigation if. . ." she hesitated.

"If what?" Danny demanded.

"If you stop calling me 'CJ.'"

He smiled and stuck out his hand to shake with her. "It's a deal."

They continued their walk up the hill to the police bungalow. Danny looked at the building with its old and peeling gray paint and thought, as he always did, that the bungalow looked a little sad.

At the door, he turned again to Crystal, "I'm supposed to meet Jade in the cafeteria for coffee in just about five minutes. I'm going to be late. Want to come?"

"Love to, but I have another class," she said.

"OK. I have to deliver these and then run on. See you later CJ, uh, Crystal." He gave her his most charming smile.

Chapter Six

Cafeteria Gossip

JADE SAT IN A corner of the college cafeteria with her psychology book open in front of her. She was waiting for Danny. There were loud conversations everywhere, along with the shouting and clatter of lunch trays and silverware. It was impossible to concentrate, so she gave up and closed the book.

The coffee she had been sipping was now cold. She made a face and pushed it away. It splashed onto the table and she wiped it up with her napkin. She ate the last bite of her bagel with cream cheese. She wanted another cup of coffee—preferably a hot one this time—but she wanted to find Danny first. Their favorite spot in the corner, farthest away from the door, was already occupied, so she had chosen seats in the opposite corner. If Danny came in and didn't see her, he might think that something had come up and she had to leave. This was their informal Wednesday morning date— coffee and bagels in the school cafeteria, and she was right on time.

Jade looked around the large room again, afraid that she had missed him. She was looking for a tall, handsome young man in a dark blue police uniform. Where was he? He was supposed to meet her right after his chemistry class, but she couldn't see him. Maybe something came up. She looked at her watch. He was ten minutes late, but she decided to give him another ten minutes.

She played with the thin gold chain on her wrist and then twisted her long hair around her fingers. She twisted her class ring around and around, then went back to twisting her hair. She was having a test in her psychology class this afternoon, and should be reviewing, but she couldn't concentrate.

She looked up when a burst of loud noise and energy came through the front door. It looked like most of the football team. They were wearing tight red pants and jerseys and carrying their helmets. The team had been practicing regularly and everybody was excited about the new season coming up. She remembered the excitement last year when they won the state championship, and people were talking about winning again this year. She thought that they wore their uniforms everywhere because they liked having the other students look at them. It was probably a matter of pride.

Even though she was not much of a football fan, she couldn't help feeling a little proud too because this winning team was from her school. She smiled and watched them as they slapped each other's backs and shouted at friends around the cafeteria. She thought they were awfully loud.

Several of them—she counted six—crowded around the long table right in front of her. She covered her ears because of the noise as they threw their books and jackets in piles on the table and, still shouting, joined the line to buy breakfast. She watched them absent-mindedly now, like a silly comedy show on TV, but they didn't seem to notice her. They were probably concentrating on breakfast. They looked hungry. They came back to the table in no time, plates piled high with eggs, sausage and toast and cups of hot coffee balanced on trays.

Joey Johnson caught sight of her and waved, gave her a big smile and winked. Tommy waved at her and shouted, "Hey, beautiful." Then they settled down to eating, joking and gossiping as if Jade were not there.

"Hey, Joey," somebody shouted from one end of the table. "Who's taking your math test for you?" Everybody at the table roared with laughter.

Jade remembered that several years before, the college had instituted a "get tough" policy on athletes. There was a front-page story in the local newspaper. All athletes were required to keep at least a C average in all classes and were not allowed any D's or F 's on their grade reports. If an athlete received failing grades, he was forced to give up playing sports until he improved his grades. At first there were a lot of surprised and unhappy athletes when they were kicked off the baseball, basketball, and football teams. The last couple of years, however, since Jade had been a student here, the athletes seemed to be taking school more seriously.

She heard the laughter die down and the group at the table became quiet. Somebody was whispering. Police training had taught her to be curious, so Jade leaned her head closer. She could catch only a few of the words and they did not make sense to her. She wrinkled her forehead in thought.

"Coach,. . . . deal. . . .easy. . . .copy."

What were they talking about? She was puzzling over this when she saw Danny, handsome in his blue uniform, come into the room.

Chapter Seven

Cafeteria Date

JADE WATCHED Danny walk confidently into the cafeteria. He looked first to their usual spot, but didn't see Jade. She waved her hand trying to catch his attention. She could see his eyes scan the large room until he found her in the opposite corner. He stepped carefully through the noisy crowd to her table. To save a place for him, she had put her backpack on the chair beside her.

"Hey, Joey. How's it going?" Danny called and waved to the captain of the football team. "Hey guys," he shouted at the players, "looks like you guys have another championship team. Good luck."

"Hey, Danny. Coming to the game Friday night? It's the big one. The first one of the season. Evergreen is a tough team. We need all the support we can get. Remember? They were the champions several years ago, three years in a row. Should be a good game."

Danny smiled. "I might. I'd love to see you dudes win for a change. You never won much when I was on the team!"

The whole team laughed and waved him away.

Danny stepped over to where Jade was sitting. He bent down and kissed her on the lips. The entire football team hooted, "Ooooh, Danny!" And several of them whistled loudly. Jade's face turned red.

Danny removed the backpack from the chair and sat down. He took her hand and looked into her dark eyes. "Want some more coffee?"

"Yes. But what is this all about? You keep telling me that I should cut down on coffee. That I drink too much."

Danny replied, "Well, you do, but it's probably better than beer and cigarettes. Do you want anything else?"

She laughed. "I already had my breakfast. You are late." She pointed her index finger at him.

"I'll tell you about it when I get back with our coffee." Danny turned and walked to the food counter at the front of the room. As he walked by the football team, they were gathering their belongings and getting ready to leave. They shouted "Goodbye" to everyone in the room and left the cafeteria the same way they came in.

The room seemed almost silent when the door closed behind them.

Jade watched Danny walking back toward her. His eyes were on the coffee, trying to balance the two cups and the bagels on the tray. She loved watching him. A strand of dark hair fell onto his forehead. He tried to blow it out of his eyes. Jade smiled. He was so handsome with those dark eyes and brown skin. He was tall and muscular. He was walking carefully through the crowd of students. He didn't spill a drop. She shook her head in admiration. He was so coordinated!

"So, why are you late?" Jade asked him as he set down their cups and put the tray aside.

Danny took a sip of his coffee before he spoke. "Captain Mitchell asked me to get those flyers from the duplicating room and deliver them to his office. And he asked me to be in charge of putting them up around the campus. He's going to assign a few students to help me out, but he put me in charge. I am also supposed to visit classes and encourage any witnesses to talk with Captain Mitchell. He told me that I was not supposed to participate in the investigation in any other way, however."

"That's great, Danny. That means he trusts you. He must know that you didn't do it."

"Do what?" he asked.

"The murder," she whispered.

"Right. Anyway." His face got serious as he told her about his new duties. He raised his hand and touched each finger as he told her the new responsibilities. "First, I'm supposed to visit classes and encourage witnesses to come forward. Second, I'm supposed to post flyers around the campus. Third, two other guys will report to me. I'm in charge of this little part of the investigation. But," he dropped his hands, "everyone tells me that nobody's going to talk, even if they did see anything. So, I guess this will be kind of a wasted effort."

"It probably won't hurt. But Danny, I want to talk to you about this murder. I don't like anyone thinking I'm a suspect. Why don't we see if we can come up with any clues?"

He looked at her lovely round face for a minute. "All right. You know the captain would have a fit if he knew what we were doing. But I agree with you. We have to do something."

Jade reached into her backpack and took out a yellow notepad and a pen. She held the pen in her hand to indicate that she was ready to start writing. With her other hand, she was twisting her hair around her fingers nervously.

"What do we know?" she asked.

Danny began to stand up to pace the floor, but Jade grabbed his hand. "No. Everybody knows that's how you solve problems. You'd better just sit here."

He nodded his head and remained seated. He started to crack his knuckles, but looked at Jade and stopped. Jade said nothing.

"Let's see," Danny began. "We can assume that she was murdered in her office. Yesterday morning before. . . What time did you get there?"

"I found her just about 7:15. I didn't look at my watch right away, but I estimate that it was just about 7:15."

Danny nodded again. "Her shoe was in the middle of the floor, so how did that happen? I would guess that the murderer had to move the body. Maybe from one side of the office to the other. The shoe fell off then. And why was it in that little space there by the bookcase. Isn't that odd? Was he trying to hide the body? Maybe he was going to put something in front of it."

"Hmm. Good question. But, it looks like she was killed in the office. That sounds right to me." Jade added this to her list of clues. "And the door was open, so it might have been someone with a key, unless she unlocked it and left it open herself."

"That's something we don't know," Danny said, "But, it looks like she was stabbed with a small object. Something like a pencil. Could you actually kill somebody with a pencil? What's something else that might be about the same size or shape?"

They were quiet for a minute, then Danny spoke again. "If the killer used a pencil, then I think the murder was not premeditated. I mean, he didn't plan to kill her. If it was a pencil, and we don't know for sure yet, then whoever did it was not planning to murder her. Maybe he or she just got mad about something. On the spot." Danny stopped talking and looked at Jade again.

Jade took up the idea where he left off. "I think you're right. I think that somebody just got mad, lost his temper and before he knew what happened, he had a dead body that he had to do something with. Hide it. I don't think he planned to kill Ms. Quinn. But, who fits that category? And why? An angry student who failed her class? Her fiancé, Mr. Taylor because, I don't know, because he was jealous? The janitor because Ms. Quinn made a mess? The janitor in Peterson Hall is kind of crazy. He doesn't speak English very well. I think he's Vietnamese. Anyway, he shouted at me once for five minutes. I had a hard time understanding him, but finally realized that he wanted me to recycle my soda can instead of throwing it in the trash."

"Ah," Danny said, "I remember that. But you know on TV, they always go after the spouse, or boyfriend, first."

"Mr. Taylor? " Jade asked. "That guy never even raises his voice.

I've never even seen him get angry at a student."

"I'm not saying it is Mr. Taylor," Danny said, "I'm just saying that we have to consider everyone. Absolutely everyone."

They sat quiet for a minute, then Danny said, "All right. Let's leave this alone for a while. Talk about it again tomorrow. We need to talk about tonight. You know, dinner."

Jade's face went white. Danny waited for her to speak. She finally said, "Are you sure you still want to do this?"

He took her hand again and felt how soft and smooth it was. He played with her slender fingers and then pressed them to his lips. Then he spoke in a calm voice. "We really need to do this now. I have been talking to my parents for several weeks. They have agreed to meet you. Dinner at our house at 7:30. I'll pick you up at 7:00."

They sat like this until Danny felt that Jade was OK. Then he went to his math class.

Chapter Eight

Mr. Taylor's Class

DANNY SAT UP straight in his chair and tried to pay attention to the dull voice of Mr. Taylor. Math shouldn't be so boring, Danny thought. Unfortunately, old man Taylor still doesn't know that. What's wrong with this guy? He used to be a better teacher. But now, he doesn't seem to care if we understand at all. He has his back to the class and he's talking to the chalkboard while he's trying to solve for x.

Danny studied the teacher's back. Mr. Taylor's dark hair was thin and always looked like he forgot to comb it. There was a large bald spot right on top of his head. His blue shirt was pulled out from his pants and one side hung down far below his belt. His dark pants had hand prints of chalk dust on the legs. Danny shook his head and straightened up again so as not to wrinkle his uniform. He ran his hand over his thick head of hair. He would be 20 years old in four months, and he wondered if he would look like Mr. Taylor some day. He certainly hoped not.

Danny took a look around the classroom. Joey, the captain of the football team, was in the back row. He had his head down on the desk, and he was snoring loudly. Next to him, Tommy was listening to music through his headphones. He had his eyes closed. Tiffany, the person everyone believed would be the next business success from Ocean View College, was dressed in her gray wool suit and white blouse. She was sitting across the aisle from Danny, and he could tell that she wasn't paying attention, either. She had her accounting book open and looked like she was studying for a test.

And Amber, sitting just in the next row behind Tiffany, was painting her fingernails a metallic black to match her eye shadow. Today she had three white stripes in her hair. It made Danny think of a zebra or a skunk. He almost laughed.

Simon, the super straight-A student, shook his head and looked angry as he put his books in his backpack and walked out the door. Mr. Taylor turned around when the door banged shut. He squinted his eyes behind thick glasses, then rubbed his broad nose, leaving a line of chalk dust on his face.

"Are there any questions?" He looked out at the room, but didn't make eye contact with any of the bored students. "If there are no questions, the test is on Friday next week."

Everybody asked in chorus, "Test? What test?"

"Well, it was supposed to be today, but Ms. Quinn's. . ." he hesitated, "uh, death has delayed the mid-term exams." He looked down at his shoes before speaking again. "If any of you has questions, I will be in my office most afternoons this week and next." Without raising his eyes, he dismissed the class.

Danny sat for a minute before gathering up his books. He stared at Mr. Taylor and silently asked himself several questions. How old is this man? Is this the way a grieving lover would act? After all, he was Ms. Quinn's fiancé. Shouldn't he be taking time off from work or something? Come to think of it, Mr. Taylor and Ms. Quinn seemed like a very odd pair. Ruby Quinn was older than Mr. Taylor, wasn't she? He guessed that Ms. Quinn was about 40. Pretty old to be getting married. Mr. Taylor looks like he might be, hmm. . . in his 30's. Maybe older. Danny cracked his knuckles while he thought.

He watched closely as Mr. Taylor gathered up his papers, erased the chalkboard and left the room. Danny sat alone in the classroom and continued thinking. And Ms. Quinn. Even though she was old, she was pretty glamorous. She always wore makeup and nice clothes. Her fingernails were always polished and her blonde hair was long and curly. As a matter of fact, he wondered, what was she doing with Mr. Taylor? What did she see in him anyway? Maybe she liked the way he did math. He almost laughed.

He stood up and headed for the door. On the way out, Danny felt a tug on his sleeve and turned to see Amber batting her eyes at him. "Hey, Danny. What's up?"

"Nothing much," he replied, not wanting to stop and talk because he was supposed to report to Captain Mitchell about his poster assignment. He was supposed to start this afternoon going around to classes and asking for information.

Amber stood there chewing on her thumbnail, one she had just painted. The snake tattoo on her wrist danced around. For just a moment, the snake wrapped around her wrist made Danny feel sorry for her because she was so weird, so odd looking. He decided he didn't need to be in such a hurry.

"What's up with you?"

"We're really busy in the duplicating office now. You know with mid-terms delayed and all. Everybody has something to be copied."

"Do you like working there?" he asked sensing there was something she wanted to say, but he didn't know what to ask.

"Oh, yeah. You know all the teachers give us their tests to be copied." She stopped talking and Danny waited. Then he cleared his throat.

"You ever get a good look at any of those tests? It must be kind of fun seeing the test before the rest of the class."

"What do you mean?" she looked afraid.

Danny looked at her and decided to proceed with caution. "Oh, like Mr. Taylor's mid-term. You see it? You heard him say we have the exam on Friday. Has he already copied it? Have you seen it? Is it hard?" He laughed to show her that he was joking, but she didn't notice.

She spoke quickly. "Yes. A lot of people have." Then she turned on her heels and nearly ran away.

Danny thought that was odd. He scratched his head and looked at his shoes. There on the ground, near the toe of his shoe was a scrap of paper. He bent down to pick it up.

He read it, but it didn't make sense. "CK 20."

He stuffed the piece of paper in his pocket and decided he should follow Amber.

Chapter Nine

Chasing Amber

DANNY RAN DOWN the hall in the science building, trying to keep his eyes on Amber. She was moving pretty fast. Students were everywhere, going to and from their morning classes. He had to move to the left and right to avoid running into people. He saw her go into the women's restroom and stopped himself before following her inside.

There was only one large door to the women's restroom, so Danny figured that she would eventually have to come out the same way she went in. He decided to wait. The hall was too crowded to pace, so he leaned against the wall and looked up and down the hall. He mumbled to himself as he waited and every few seconds looked toward the restroom door. He didn't want to miss her. He was completely lost in thought when he felt a hand on his shoulder. It was Coach Kelly.

"Hey, Danny. What's the matter? You have a fugitive trapped in there?"

Danny managed a little smile. "No, Coach. Just waiting for someone."

"She must be some girl if you can't stand to have her out of your sight for a minute."

"No, Coach. It's not like that. I. . ." But Danny didn't finish the sentence because the coach had already moved on down the hall.

Danny continued his survey of the hall. He looked toward the men's room, which was through the next door, and saw Mr. Taylor coming out. His hair looked just as messy as ever. Danny thought anyone going into a room with a mirror should at least take a quick look at himself. Mr. Taylor apparently didn't think the same way. Danny smoothed out his hair again with his hand.

"Hey, Danny." He turned around when he heard Amber call his name.

"Oh, Amber. You're just the person I wanted to see. Do you have a class now, or do you have time for a cup of coffee? I'm buying."

One look at her face and Danny could tell that she looked both surprised and very happy.

"I can't. I have to go to work in the Duplicating Office. Like, right now. How about another time? A rain check?"

He fell into step beside her as she walked toward Peterson Hall. He thought about the little scrap of paper. Amber probably dropped it. What did it mean? Why did she seem so frightened when he asked about the math test? He might as well ask.

He reached in his pocket and pulled out the piece of paper and held it out toward her.

"I think you dropped this."

Amber grabbed it from his hand instantly and stuffed it in her own pocket.

They walked along in silence a few more steps, then Danny spoke.

"What was that?" he asked casually.

"Just, just something for my job. No big deal."

Danny nodded, but changed the subject. "You know, Amber, I have been meaning to ask you about that football game. You going with anyone?"

She stopped suddenly, turned to look him in the face and asked, "You want to go with me, Danny?" Her eyes were wide and her face showed just the beginning of a smile.

"Well, uh, when is it? This Friday or next?" he asked.

"This Friday. Be ready at 6:30. I'll pick you up." She was smiling broadly again.

Danny hesitated only for a second. Then he smiled. "Well, uh, OK. Friday it is."

He left Amber at the door of the Duplicating Office and it suddenly hit him. "I have a date with Amber. Oh, God," he said and slapped his hand against his forehead, "I have a date with Amber! I have to tell Jade. No. She wouldn't understand. Yes. I have to tell her or she'll think I'm really cheating. No. She's always been jealous of Amber. She wouldn't understand." He slapped himself again. "Oh, God, how am I going to pull this off? Stupid. Really stupid. I have a date with Amber." He groaned.

By the time he reached the police bungalow, he had decided that it was better if Jade didn't know about this little date with Amber—at least not right away. Maybe in about ten years. Or maybe never.

Chapter Ten

Dinner at Danny's

JADE STOOD AT the big front window looking out. She could see her reflection in the window. She was wearing a white silk dress that hung to her ankles. Her shoes were white with silver buckles on the toes for decoration. Her long black hair was twisted and pinned on the top of her head and there were chopsticks with pearl handles stuck through her hair. She touched the string of pearls around her neck and the little pearl earrings in her ears. On her right hand was a pearl ring set in gold.

She checked her watch and bit her lip, folded and unfolded her hands, crossed her arms over her chest and then uncrossed them. She checked her watch again. It was 7:20. She sat down and stood up and sat down again. She looked down the street to the left, then down the street to the right and frowned. Danny is late again, she thought while staring at her watch.

At 7:25, he drove his white Mustang—12 years old, clean, but with dents in the fender—into the driveway and hopped out. As soon as he rang the bell, Jade opened the door and grabbed his arm in a tight grip.

"Wow! You look great!" Danny said and then smiled his approval and gave her a quick kiss. He looked at her frown and asked, "What's wrong? My parents will like you! They have to. You're 19, you're beautiful and I love you. What's not to like?"

The corners of her mouth turned up in the tiniest smile and she loosened her grip on his arm just a little. Danny picked up her coat, looked at the grip on his arm and told her, "If you want to wear this coat, you're going to have to let go of my arm for just a minute."

She did, then told him that she had to speak to her mother before they left. Jade left Danny and went back to the kitchen where her mother was. They were speaking in Chinese so she knew Danny wouldn't understand the words. She was glad of that. Her mother didn't want her going out with Danny, but she didn't feel that she could always be the dutiful daughter.

When she returned, she noticed that Danny looked worried, but didn't ask about it. Instead, she let Danny open the door for her, help her into the car and fasten the seatbelt. He got in, started the engine and backed out of the driveway. Jade let out her breath and they sat in silence for the first few blocks. While they rode across town, Jade quizzed herself on his family. "Your brothers are Johnny and Carlos? Your sisters are Gloria and Rosa?" she asked.

"Right," Danny said.

"Carlos is older than you? The girls are younger?"

"Right again." He turned his head to look at her while they were waiting for the red light to change. He squeezed her hand and winked.

"Relax. You're doing fine." He smiled.

"I'm so nervous. We've been trying to set up this meeting for almost a year. I don't want to blow it now."

"We won't."

As they pulled into the Soto family's driveway, Jade could see young faces in a cluster at the front window. And before Danny could park the car, she saw the front door burst open and two young people tumbled out to greet them.

When they walked in, her ears immediately caught the loud salsa music coming from a stereo somewhere in a back room. She looked around. There were family pictures on tables and on the walls. Above the fireplace, there was a picture of Jesus on a big wooden cross. Jade remembered that Mr. and Mrs. Soto were very religious.

Danny introduced his siblings. Johnny wore shiny black pants and a pale blue shirt. He looked about 16, and Jade thought he looked like he was ready to go dancing. He smiled, took her hand and kissed it. Gloria was wearing a large white flower in her long reddish hair. Carlos wore glasses and was quiet and shy, but Jade could tell that he liked her. Carlos was only a year older than Danny, if she remembered correctly. Rosa was only eight and very excited. She took Jade's hand and jumped up and down, saying, "I'm going to sit by you!"

Danny led Jade into the kitchen to meet his mother. Jade looked around quickly at the dishes and mess in the kitchen and her nose caught the scent of something wonderful cooking. In front of the stove, stood Mrs. Soto, a short, round woman with graying hair. The older woman wiped her hands on her old blue apron, nodded to Jade, said "Hello," and smiled politely but that was all. She did not start a conversation. Danny took Jade's hand and led her out of the hot kitchen.

Jade bit her lip then coughed nervously. She wondered where Mr. Soto was. Could he be hiding? She put her arms around Danny's neck and pulled him closer so that she could whisper in his ear. "Where is your father?"

"Probably in his workshop. He'll be in. Why are you whispering? It's OK. You are allowed to talk."

Jade giggled nervously but tried to relax. They proceeded to the living room. She heard the music as they got nearer. She saw that somebody had rolled back the carpet from the floor leaving a wide space in the middle of the room. The space was just right for dancing. They watched Johnny teaching Rosa to dance.

"Back. Forward. To the left. Faster. Good."

The others gave advice from the sidelines. "Listen to the rhythm. Take smaller steps. Turn around."

Soon Gloria and Carlos got up and started to dance. Then Danny asked Jade if she would like to dance with him.

"Of course." She smiled and they joined the others on the living room dance floor.

When Mrs. Soto came in to announce dinner, Jade looked at her watch and noticed that it was already 8:15. She remembered that dinner was supposed to be at 7:30. She's late, like Danny, she thought. Maybe it's a family tradition. A late dinner didn't bother her, though, because she wasn't really very hungry. The party moved toward the dining room and as they turned the corner, Jade took in wonderful smells coming from a very full table.

She was just a little surprised to see a handsome older man already sitting at the head of the long table. Danny introduced Jade to his father. Jade smiled and looked at Mr. Soto. She could see an older version of Danny. The older man stood up and held out his hand to shake hers, then told everyone to be seated. He did not smile and this made Jade nervous again. She took her seat between Danny and Rosa.

After praying over the food, Mr. Soto picked up a platter of tamales and held it for Jade while she served herself. Then she helped Rosa and passed the platter to Danny. After her plate was filled with salad, beans, rice and tamales, she took a deep breath and decided that everything was going to be OK. She quickly changed her mind, however, when Mr. Soto looked right at her and spoke, "Danny tells me that your family is from Hong Kong. How long have you been here in California?"

"I was just a baby when they immigrated," Jade replied.

"You know, we are all citizens here, even though we immigrated from Mexico." Mr. Soto continued, "and we have kept our customs from Mexico. Danny was born here, so he knows a lot about American ways, but his mother and I enjoy the old traditions of Mexico. And we are Catholic."

Jade sucked in her breath and looked right at Mr. Soto. "I, too, am a citizen. I became a naturalized citizen many years ago. My parents also taught me the old traditional Chinese ways. My father passed away a couple of years ago, so now it's just my mother and me. We keep the Chinese traditions." She grabbed Danny's hand and closed her mouth tight, afraid that she had already said too much. What about the Catholic church? Would his parents be very upset that she was not Catholic? Should she become Catholic? Could she?

She looked around the table at Danny's siblings. Carlos had his eyes directly on his plate. He looked afraid. Johnny looked angry. Rosa's eyes were as big as the dinner plates.

Danny tried to distract everyone from the tension around the table. He told a joke about a dog and a fire hydrant. Nobody laughed. Then he started talking about the murder at Ocean View College. Slowly, everyone turned eyes on Danny, but the tension in the air was very heavy for the rest of the meal.

Chapter Eleven

Crystal and Jade

JADE SAT IN her corner of the cafeteria, waiting for Crystal. Her coffee cup was empty again, but she didn't want any more. She took a long strand of hair and twirled it around her finger. She twirled and twirled and thought. Her eyes were almost closed and her lips turned down at the corners.

"Hey there, girl. What's got you all in a knot?"

Jade jerked her eyes open at the sound of Crystal's voice and she smiled for the first time all morning. "I never could fool you, Crys."

"OK. So don't even try!" Crystal pointed her long slender brown finger at Jade and winked. "Either you are very tired or very worried. Which one is it? You've got that hair going around your finger so fast my eyes can hardly follow." Crystal turned her head in circles to indicate that she was getting dizzy, then shook her finger at Jade.

Jade laughed. "All right! All right! I'm upset. I couldn't sleep last night!"

Crystal looked straight at her and said, "I would bet this has something to do with your dinner last night with Danny's family."

"You know me too well, Crys."

"So, are you going to tell me about it, or do I have to drag it out of you? And you know I can do that. I'm an ace interrogator!"

Jade laughed again. "That you are." She took a deep breath then said simply. "They didn't like me. They didn't like me at all." Her lips quivered as if she were going to cry. "His father made it clear that they are from Mexico and I am not. He told me he was a citizen. Does he think I'm an illegal alien and want to marry Danny for a green card? But Danny told me his father especially has been against us since the beginning. Danny doesn't even think he has a real reason."

Crystal looked at her before saying anything else. Then she spoke softly. "You knew that was a possibility. You told me that yourself. You know how these old traditional families are. They want their kids to marry people just like them. In this case, the Soto family would prefer that Danny's girlfriend speak some

Spanish, know how to cook tamales and have long black hair—
which you have unless you twist it all out of your head the way
you're doing right now."

Jade quickly pulled her fingers from her hair and folded her
hands in front of her on the table.

She spoke in a calm voice, "Of course, I understand this because
my mother is acting the same way. In fact, I couldn't even tell her
about Danny for the first six months that we were dating. I was
afraid of what she would say."

"She knows now, doesn't she?" Crystal asked.

Jade nodded her head.

"And what does she say?" Crystal continued her interrogation.

Jade took a deep breath and let it out quickly. "She won't even
talk to me about Danny, except to say that I shouldn't be dating
him. Every time I try to bring it up, try to tell her how I feel, my
mother turns and walks out of the room."

Crystal thought for a minute. "Then, actually, Mr. and Mrs. Soto
are a little bit ahead of your mother. They let Danny invite you over
to share a meal with them. Your mother won't even talk about the
two of you."

Jade took in another deep breath and let it out quickly. "I know
that. But we were just hoping. We were hoping that if the Sotos
would accept me that maybe my mother would soften up a little."

She looked across the table and noticed a touch of sadness in
Crystal's eyes. "Crys, has anything like this ever happened to you?"

Crystal closed her eyes and sat quietly as if she were far away in
another world. Then she opened her eyes and began to speak slowly. "It was about three years ago. I was crazy about this guy. He
worked at the modeling agency. A cameraman. We dated for several
months before I had the courage to tell my mother. I invited him
home and my mother yelled at me for a week. She kept asking me if
I knew what I was getting mixed up with, dating a white guy. She
said that I was just asking for trouble."

"And?" Jade prompted her to continue.

"Tony—the guy—couldn't take it. He broke it off. I was devastat-
ed."

"Is that," Jade started hesitatingly, "is that when you left Los
Angeles?"

Crystal nodded without speaking.

"And you haven't been back?"

Crystal nodded again silently.

Tears formed in Jade's eyes.

The two young women sat quietly for a few minutes until Crystal
broke the silence. "Hey, girl, I have a favor to ask you. Could you

trade with me tomorrow night? I'm on the schedule to direct traffic and patrol at the football game. But I have a date. If you do this for me, I'll take your traffic duty any morning next week. Your choice."

"Well, I don't have a date, so I might as well. And have a good time." Jade finally smiled.

Chapter Twelve

Riding with Amber

DANNY WAS IN front of his house looking up and down the street and waiting for Amber. He chose to wait outside because he didn't want his older brother to get suspicious. The family, except for Carlos and Danny, were all in church. Carlos was studying in his room upstairs. Danny didn't want Carlos to know that he had a date with someone else tonight—someone who wasn't Jade. He didn't know how to explain. He wasn't sure he understood it himself.

Danny was wearing blue jeans and a red t-shirt. He knew that Amber liked his police uniform, but he wanted to blend into the crowd as much as possible and not attract attention. He knew that someone might see him with Amber and the news would get back to Jade, but he hoped to delay that news. He would worry about telling her later. He had other things to worry about right now.

Danny waited and paced, waited and paced. This was his first date with anybody except Jade in over a year, and it wasn't like he really wanted to go. As he walked back and forth waiting for Amber, he talked to himself. He formed a fist with his left hand and punched his right hand every time he made a point in this conversation.

"Amber has information." His fist slapped against his palm. "I'm sure of that." Another hit against his hand. "There's something going on in the duplicating office." Another hit. I want that information." Another hit. "When I asked her about the tests, she looked nervous. She ran away. It's something about the tests and teachers. But what?" He hit his palm again. "There is something going on in that office. I want to know what it is." He punched his hand hard and cried, "Ouch!"

He was so busy talking to himself that he forgot to check the street traffic, so he looked up in surprise when he heard a car horn honk. Amber parked right in front of the house.

He cracked his knuckles and rolled his head to loosen up before the evening, which he felt was going to be awkward and uncomfortable.

There was Amber. She was dressed in tight red jeans and a tight red sweater that showed off her oversized figure. Her dark hair was teased high up on her head with three strawberry-red stripes running back from her forehead. There was a little red ribbon pinned on top. Her short fingernails were painted blood red and she wore bright red lipstick. On her feet, she wore three-inch spike-heeled shoes—red.

"Hey, Danny," she smiled and gave him a wink. Danny smiled weakly. He thought she looked like a red traffic light. STOP! This made him really smile.

Danny sat in the passenger seat of Amber's almost brand new car. He wondered where she had gotten the money to buy it. She was a student, after all, and students, he knew, were usually poor. He tried to fasten the seatbelt, but discovered that it was broken. He held it across his chest in a tight grip.

Amber put the car in gear and tore out onto the street and almost hit a city bus, which was passing by. Danny sucked in his breath. He wanted to make it back home alive. Then again, if they died in a car crash, he wouldn't have to explain this date to Jade.

"Hey, Amber, what happened to the seatbelt here?"

"Well," she turned to look at him as she talked and somebody honked a horn at her. She paid no attention. "I almost had a little accident about a week ago. Tiffany was sitting there and I had to stop really fast. She hit the windshield. She's OK, but it tore that thing loose and I haven't had a chance to get it fixed. Good brakes on this car, though. Really good."

"What about the airbags?"

"Oh, I guess they don't work."

Danny took a deep breath and thought, great. No airbags, either.

Danny didn't know what to say, so he just held his breath and tried not to be afraid. He hoped she was right about the brakes.

Amber talked all the way to the Ocean View College campus. She lifted her hands off the steering wheel to emphasize her words. She ran a red light and rolled through a stop sign. Danny began to wish that he had gone to church with his parents. He thought he needed to pray right about now. Amber just kept on talking. Danny said nothing, but wondered if he had the authority to give her a ticket for running the red light or for speeding. Maybe if he had worn his uniform, she might have paid more attention to her driving.

When they pulled into the student parking lot at school, Danny felt a headache coming on. He closed his eyes and rubbed his temples with both hands. He took in a deep breath and wondered what Jade was doing just then. He wished he could be doing it with her—whatever it was.

Jade stood at the main entrance of the student parking lot. She blew her whistle and raised her hand to stop a line of cars ready to drive into the lot. She waved to another line of cars signaling for the drivers to come forward. She stopped the cars to allow pedestrians to cross the street. She repeated these motions over and over again—stop and go, stop and go—until her arms were tired and her throat felt sore.

She hated working traffic at football games, but this was a favor to Crystal and Jade looked forward to Crystal taking one of her mornings next week. Which one? She wondered now. She hated getting up in the morning, so Crystal's offer was almost like winning the lottery. Since she had not heard from Danny about a date tonight, she thought this was a good way to keep busy. Maybe after that dinner at their house his parents told him not to see her any more. She tried not to think about that.

Besides the morning off and trying to keep busy, Jade thought this good deed and taking this responsibility would give Captain Mitchell a good impression of her. She wanted to stay on the right side of Captain Mitchell. The investigation of Ms. Quinn's death was not over yet, and Jade was not sure if her name had been erased from the list of suspects.

It seemed like hundreds of cars were looking for parking in the student parking lot. Cars and more cars raced past her as she stood with her whistle in her mouth and her arms motioning to stop and go. Most of the vehicles were just a blur before her eyes, but when she saw a fancy red sports car with Amber at the wheel and someone who looked a lot like Danny in the passenger seat, she dropped her whistle and stared. He had his hands over his face. Was he hiding?

Chapter Thirteen

Touchdown

DANNY'S HEAD was spinning. Amber drove her little red car like a jet plane. She sped around the parking lot, talking constantly, and finally she decided on two parking spaces near the south end of the huge parking area. He watched as she parked between the two spaces so that some other poor student looking for a space would be out of luck.

Danny hopped out of the car and felt himself shaking from the wild ride. He was glad to put his feet on solid ground again. He liked driving fast, but this was a little too scary.

Amber was chattering away, but he was not paying attention to anything she was saying. Maybe he should, but he just couldn't concentrate right now. He grabbed her elbow when she started running toward the main gate and the crowded path to the football field. He saw the crowd of students heading in that direction and decided he wasn't ready to be recognized by anyone yet.

"Hey, Amber, let's go out this way. It's less crowded." He pointed to a narrow bike path that led around the Science Hall and eventually to the football field.

She flashed him a big smile and winked. "Why Danny, you devil! You just want to be alone with me." She hooked her arm in his and continued chattering as they walked toward the Science Hall.

She was laughing and waving her arms as they entered the gate to the football stadium. She took Danny's hand and pulled him as she made her way through the crowd on the bleachers. He wondered where she was taking him, but didn't ask. She did not stop talking for a second. She pushed her way to the section closest to the Ocean View team where they could have a good view of the field and the cheerleaders.

Amber stepped on someone's feet and Danny apologized for her. Her large bag knocked over a soda, but she kept on walking. Danny felt his face getting red from embarrassment. She finally stopped and let go of Danny's hand. He guessed that these were the seats she was heading for all along. They were taken. She put her hands on her hips and looked at the two young students who must have been freshmen. She spoke in a loud voice over the noise of the crowd.

"Excuse me, but these seats are reserved. You will have to move." The two looked at Amber, and Danny could see on their faces that they decided they could not win an argument with this large woman dressed all in red. They moved away quietly. Danny shook his head and thought that one day somebody would probably explain to them that there are no reserved seats in these bleachers.

Danny looked at the ground. His face was hot and his tongue wouldn't move. He didn't know what he might say anyway.

Once they sat down, Amber turned to Danny and asked if he wanted a hot dog. Before he could answer, she added, "My treat."

Danny cleared his throat, "Well, uh, thanks anyway, but I had a big dinner." She frowned briefly and continued talking. He could feel his headache coming back. He closed his eyes and rubbed his temples, but Amber continued to chatter. She barely stopped to get her breath. Then he noticed that she was talking about the football team. He opened his eyes and focused on her, trying to listen. She talked about each one—who they were dating, where they planned to transfer when the semester was over and which ones were having trouble staying on the team because of their grades.

Danny's ears perked up at the mention of grades. Grades, tests, teachers? How did Amber know so much? He remembered how she ran away when he asked about the math test. She had looked nervous. What did she know about these tests? He focused his eyes trying to form a question. What could he ask her?

"Did you say Joey Johnson is having trouble with math? He's in my math class. With Mr. Taylor. He doesn't seem to pay attention in class, but he seems to do all right on the tests, as far as I know. Anyway, he's playing football and we all know that he wouldn't be if he didn't have a C average."

Amber closed her mouth quickly. She bit her lip. She looked like maybe she was embarrassed about saying too much.

Danny smiled at her. "Just curious, you know. I always wonder how other people manage to keep up their grades and play sports. I always had trouble with that. That's why I didn't try out for the team this year. Since I'm planning to take the exam to enter the Police Academy, my GPA is very important right now."

Amber looked at him cautiously from behind her long black eye lashes. "Maybe he gets some help. Maybe a tutor. Or, I don't know." She shut her mouth again.

But Danny thought she did know something. He looked over at her and she was chewing on her thumbnail. She was nervous. "Who do they get for tutoring and how much does it cost? Maybe I can get some help, too. I'm having a little trouble with math."

She looked at Danny again, this time showing some worry on her face. "Coach Kelly tries to help out the team. You know, he doesn't want to lose anyone. If they don't keep up their grades, they have to give up playing sports. That's the law now, you know."

Danny didn't know where to go from here. "Do you think if I talked to Coach Kelly he could help me, too?"

Amber put her hand on Danny's leg and leaned closer to him. The snake tattoo on her wrist danced as she whispered, "I don't think you want this kind of help, Danny."

"Why not?" His eyes were wide and he tried to ignore the hand on his thigh.

She put her arm around Danny's neck and pulled his face closer. She put her lips to his ear and whispered again. "It's a secret. You have to promise. You can't tell a soul."

Danny's heart started to pound. Without thinking, he whispered back, "I promise."

"He buys tests."

Danny sat very still, then asked, "Who?"

"The coach," she whispered. Then she pulled him even closer and kissed his cheek, leaving a big red lip print for everybody around to admire.

Chapter Fourteen

Fumble

JADE STOOD stone still at the entrance to the parking lot. She was
sure that Danny and Amber had just sped by in a red car. Jade was
stunned. Cars continued to zoom by her with loud music coming
from their windows. Somebody honked a horn and she jerked herself back to reality. She grabbed her whistle and blew. She raised
her arms to the approaching cars, directing traffic with great energy, which came from the anger rising inside her. With every arm
movement and every whistle blow, she got angrier. When the last
car drove into the lot, she was exhausted and wanted nothing more
than to go home and crawl into her own warm bed. But the evening
wasn't over. She had to stay until the game was over and make sure
everybody was safe and every car left the parking lot.

Her head began to ache and she rubbed her scalp and her temples, and she wondered what to do next. That was Danny. There
was no mistaking him. And that was Amber. Everybody could recognize Amber! So that was why he hadn't called! That is why she
didn't have a date tonight! Amber had been chasing him as long as
she could remember. It looks like she finally caught him! Jade
groaned. What now?

She straightened her shoulders and took a deep breath. Part of
her job this evening was to patrol the crowd in the bleachers to
make sure nobody had drugs or alcohol and to try to stop any
fights that might break out. She didn't feel up to it tonight. But duty
is duty and this was hers. She started walking in the direction of
the stadium and the roar of the crowd.

She came in through the gate and wasn't sure how much of the
game she had missed. She looked up at the scoreboard: nothing to
nothing. She wondered if the game had just started. She took another deep breath and took a quick look around the bleachers at the
crowd of people. They were mostly students and mostly from
Ocean View College. Many people were wearing red and white, the
school colors. From here, everything looked all right. The seats
were filled. She started up the steps to the bleachers to take a walk
up and down the aisles, checking out the action. She was half hop-

ing that she would not see Danny and Amber. The other half wanted to get mad again. And she knew seeing them together would really make her mad.

Half of her wish came true. In the section nearest the home team's cheerleaders, she spotted them. She stopped dead in her tracks. She was far enough away that they couldn't see her, and anyway, it didn't look like either of them cared whether she was there or not. Amber had her arms around Danny's neck and it looked like she was whispering something in his ear. Jade's eyes grew wider as she watched Amber plant a big kiss on Danny's cheek. Jade turned her head quickly and bit her lip to stop the tears ready to spill out from her eyes. She started walking faster to get away. They still hadn't seen her. She gripped the wooden baton hanging from her belt until her knuckles turned white. She could feel herself getting angrier, ready to explode. She walked to the end of the bleachers and down under the scoreboard.

There was a fence part way around the area and she thought she could hide for at least a few minutes. She knew that she needed to cool off. Instead of walking around the entire seating area, as she usually would, she stayed at the end farthest away from Danny and Amber. She looked around every few minutes trying to spot trouble, but she didn't see any—except for Amber and the hands she had all over Danny. She wasn't close enough to see Danny's face, so she couldn't tell whether he was enjoying himself or not. She tried not to pay any attention to them, but she just couldn't help herself. Her eyes kept returning to the two of them, sitting near the goal posts. She bit her lip and narrowed her eyes. "If I didn't have to be on duty tonight," she spoke quietly to herself, "I would, uh... What would I do? Go out for revenge! Get both of them! Those dirty rats! Scum bags! Slime balls!"

For the rest of the evening, she performed her duties the best she could under the circumstances. When the game was just about over, she left the stadium and returned to the parking lot. She didn't even know the score. She hadn't been paying attention to anything happening on the field. She hadn't been watching the scoreboard or listening to the cheers from the crowd. She was thinking about revenge.

Chapter Fifteen

More Questions, More Trouble

DANNY LISTENED to Amber and thought about what she was saying. The coach was buying tests. He was buying them for his team so that they could pass their academic classes and continue to play sports. This information brought a lot of questions with it. If the coach is buying tests, then who is selling? Amber? And does this have anything to do with Ms. Quinn's murder? Did the coach murder Ms. Quinn? Did she find out about this little test-buying scheme? Is that why she was killed?
Is that a good enough reason to kill somebody?

He was deep in thought and not watching the game very closely. When everyone around him started to cheer, he looked up at the scoreboard and realized that Ocean View College had made a touchdown. He cheered, too. Then he became aware of Amber's arm around his neck. His face felt hot. He was embarrassed. He hoped that no one he knew saw him like this. What if someone told Jade? He would really be in trouble then. He took Amber's arm and removed it from around his neck. She looked hurt, so he took her hand and held it. It was better this way. He wouldn't have to worry about her grabbing his leg. She looked at him and winked. She made little kissing motions with her lips. Danny tried to ignore this. He tried to think of the right questions to ask her. After all, getting information was the reason that he had made this date.

"Uh, Amber," he tried to speak quietly, "where does the coach buy these tests?"

She looked at him for a second. He thought he saw fear in her eyes. Finally, she pulled him closer and whispered in his ear. "I can't tell you that, Danny. It's the amendment thing."

At first, he was puzzled. He didn't know what she was talking about. Then he realized it was the Fifth Amendment to the Constitution. If she answered the question, she might become a suspect, too. He thought for a minute. "You don't have anything to do with it, do you?"

Amber didn't answer. She just looked at him and her eyes said, "Don't ask any more questions." She turned her eyes to the game.

Danny usually found football interesting, but tonight he was not interested at all in the game. He decided that he would wait before asking her any more questions. His mind kept racing and his eyes moved around the bleachers looking for something. He didn't know what. Just then, he saw a familiar figure dressed in the student police uniform. It was Jade! Her back was turned to him and she was walking away. Oh, no! Did she see them? She was only a few feet away. How could she miss them? Where was she going? He could feel his face get hot and sweat break out on his forehead. Now what? How was he ever going to get out of this one?

Chapter Sixteen

Sleepless Night

DANNY AND AMBER left the football game in the middle of the crowd, and when they were in the parking lot, Danny suggested that they drive on the bike path, which joined the main road just outside the exit gates. He wanted to avoid seeing Jade again, and he knew she would be at the main entrance. He felt a little guilty making the suggestion, but he felt guilty about a lot of things tonight.

Once out of the parking lot, Amber sped on down Main Street, talking a mile a minute. Danny nodded his head once in a while but was generally lost in his own thoughts.

"Danny," he heard his name and looked over at Amber. "Danny, what's wrong with you? I've asked you three times if you want to stop at the Burger Barn for something to eat. Where are you anyway? Well?" Amber's eyebrows went up and she wrinkled her forehead.

"Oh, sorry. No, I'm really not hungry. I need to get on home. I promised my dad I would help him with some work around the house tomorrow. Have to get up early."

Amber was silent, obviously not pleased. They rode the rest of the way to Danny's house without talking. When they pulled into the driveway, Amber put on the brake and turned to Danny. He already had his hand on the door handle, ready to jump out and away from this woman.

"Wait, Danny."

He turned back to her and tried to smile. "Thanks, Amber, for the ride, and I enjoyed the game. It's nice to win for a change. We did win, didn't we?"

She laughed. "Danny, you are too funny! Of course, we won!" Then she grabbed his shirt and pulled him close to her, and before he could move away, she kissed him again—this time square on the lips. He caught his breath and hurried out of the car. He went into the house without looking back.

The house was quiet, fortunately. He really didn't want to talk to anyone just now. He had a lot of thinking to do. In his room, he started to pace, back and forth from the door to the desk, from the desk to the door. Jade, Coach Kelly, the football team, Amber, tests, cheating. Where should he start? He cracked his knuckles then he pulled at his hair.

He stopped suddenly. This wasn't helping. Pulling his hair didn't pull any answers out of his brain. He lay down on the bed and stared at the ceiling. That didn't help, either. He got up again and took a piece of paper and a pen from the desk. He wrote at the top of the page, "What to do about." Then he drew three lines down the page, dividing the page into columns. At the top of the first column, he wrote "Jade." At the top of the second column, he wrote "Coach Kelly." At the top of the third column, he wrote "Amber."

For the next hour, Danny wrote down ideas on how to handle all of his problems. When he finally closed his eyes, he was able to sleep.

Chapter Seventeen

Midnight Caller

JADE LEFT the stadium before the final touchdown was scored and returned to the parking lot. She wanted to walk around the lot at least once to check for vandalism and alcohol or drug use. She glanced at her watch and noticed that it was almost 11:00 p.m. She wondered when this night would be over and she could go home and call Crystal. She needed to talk to someone.

The parking lot was lit around the edges by large spotlights, but in the center of the area, it was dark. She carried her police issue flashlight and began walking up and down the aisles of the big lot. On aisle five, she heard some activity somewhere in the middle. She had patrolled this lot at night before and nothing had ever happened to make her afraid, but she was on her guard as she had been taught in her classes.

As she got closer, she lifted her flashlight and was ready to point the light in the direction of the noise, when she was blinded. Someone flashed a light directly in her face. She closed her eyes and shouted, "Turn it off. Police!" The light did not leave her face. She tried to step out of the way of the blinding light beam, but it followed her. She shouted again, "Turn it off! Police!"

"Start it up, Tom," a male voice shouted. Jade heard an engine start with a roar, a door slam and then a car speed away. The light was finally gone, but it took a few seconds before she could see again.

"What was that all about? Who was that? What were they doing that they didn't want me to know about? And, damn, they got away!" She was shouting at no one.

She stood there a minute trying to think through what had just happened and what, if anything, she should do about it. Well, nobody was hurt. There was no damage as far as she knew. Would Captain Mitchell like to know about this? She decided to write up an incident report to give him on Monday. It didn't seem serious. She shook her head and continued on her way.

It was almost midnight when the last car left the parking lot, but Jade wasn't tired. She was too angry and hurt to be tired. She didn't think she could sleep. She got into her car and punched in Crystal's number on her cell phone. There was no answer, so she left a short message. "Call me when you get home. It doesn't matter how late it is." She didn't think to identify herself.

She drove home, parked the car and hurried to her room. Thank God her mother wasn't awake. There was no one else around the house to disturb these days. She was glad to be alone.

As she lay in bed staring at the ceiling, her cell phone rang. She hit "talk" and heard Crystal's pleasant voice.

"Hey, girl. What's up? You didn't sound so good on that little message you left me."

"It's Danny." Jade said sharply. "And Amber."

"What? What do you mean?"

"I saw them together. At the game. She kissed him! She kissed him right there in front of God and everybody! I saw it!" Jade had to slow down to take a breath.

Crystal was quiet for a second before she asked, "Can you think of any logical explanation?"

"Hell, no!"

"I didn't think so. Now, what are you going to do about it?"

I don't know yet, but I'm mad. Really steamed. They deserve each other. She looks like a skunk and he is one."

"I can tell you're mad," said Crystal, "because you don't usually swear."

"Don't you think this situation calls for a little swearing?" Jade raised her voice, then lowered it again when she remembered that her mother was asleep.

Crystal said, "Absolutely!" and Jade could hear a little smile in her voice.

"If you hadn't had a date tonight. . ." Jade stopped in the middle of her sentence, then changed the subject abruptly. "Oh, how was your date? Where did you go? Do you think you'll see him again? Details. I want all the details."

Crystal laughed and Jade started to smile, too. Crystal had a great laugh.

"We had dinner at the Oak Tree Restaurant. You know, that fancy new one downtown. The food was good. Then we took a walk. Then. . ."

Jade interrupted her. "I want to know what he's like. Start with the physical."

Crystal laughed again. "His name is Brian. He's tall, dark and handsome, of course. He's a student at State University, and he should graduate this semester. He's majoring in business and plans to have lots of money one day soon."

"Good. Good. And did you like him?" Jade asked a little impatiently.

"I did. We have another date next weekend." Crystal was quiet again for just a moment, then she changed the subject. "Now, to get back to Danny, Amber and the football game that I missed. Just what are you going to do about this? Did either of them see you?"

"I don't think so. And as for what I should do now, I don't know yet. Got any ideas?"

"Well, Crystal said slowly, "we could tie him to the goal post on the football field and leave him all night. Naked. Turn on the sprinklers." They both laughed and promised to think about revenge and talk again in the morning. Jade hung up with a sigh and returned to staring at the ceiling.

Chapter Eighteen

Danny Solves Problems

OVER THE weekend, Danny tried to call Jade on her cell phone three times, but she didn't answer and she didn't call him back. He figured that she must have seen him with Amber at the football game. On Saturday, he went to the florist in the neighborhood and ordered a dozen red roses to be delivered to Jade. Most of the weekend, however, he spent helping his father around the house. They were painting the kitchen. He also spent a lot of time thinking about his problems.

By Sunday evening he had a plan, or actually several plans.

First he was going to talk to Mr. Taylor about his math. He wanted to see if he could pick up any information about these stolen tests or clues on how it worked. He actually was having a little trouble with math anyway, so he wouldn't have to make up an excuse, and he remembered Mr. Taylor inviting anyone with questions to visit him in his office.

Next was Amber. He certainly didn't want to go out with her again, but he was sure that she had the rest of the information that he needed. Somehow the test stealing business fit into this murder case. He didn't know how, but he wanted to find out. He decided that Crystal was the perfect choice. She could get information out of a stone wall, and anyway, she already knew something about the case. And he could trust her. Besides, that would fit into the solution of the third problem—Jade. Because she was Jade's best friend, he was sure that he could pass information from Crystal to Jade, especially since Jade had not been picking up her phone when he called. She had not called to thank him for the roses.

On Monday morning, Danny set his plans in motion. He arrived on campus early and went to Peterson Hall. He hoped to talk to Mr. Taylor. When he got to the seventh floor, he saw that Mr. Taylor was not in. He checked the schedule posted beside the door and found out that he would be in his office that afternoon at 1:00. Good. He would come back then. He decided that he should prepare some questions to ask just so he wouldn't get in there, sit silent like a stone and look stupid.

When he left Peterson Hall, he went up the hill to the Criminal Justice bungalow. He hoped to catch Crystal before she got too busy. On the way, he thought about what he would tell her. Danny was reaching out his hand to open the door when it flew open and a tall, dark woman rushed out almost knocking him down.

"Danny," Crystal sounded surprised. "Sorry."

"CJ, just the person I was looking for."

She squinted her eyes at him and tightened her jaw.

"Oh, sorry. Crystal. I forgot. It might take me some time to remember that."

"Well, we had a deal and you promised. You can't call me CJ anymore. Anyway, why are you looking for me?" she asked.

"I need your help." He looked her in the eye but didn't say anything else.

Crystal stared back at him. "With what?"

"Do you have time? Can we go somewhere and talk now? It's important." Danny pleaded.

She stared at him a second before answering. "All right. How about the cafeteria?"

"No. I don't want anyone to hear us. We need some privacy."

"OK. How about the squad car? I'm on duty pretty soon. It won't hurt to start a little early. You can ride along."

Danny agreed and followed her to the college police car parked outside the bungalow. They got in and Crystal drove slowly toward the gymnasium at the south end of the campus. She looked at Danny and said, "So, talk."

He cleared his throat. "Well," he stuttered, "I want you to investigate Amber."

"Investigate Amber? Why?"

"Well, you see," Danny started again, "Coach Kelly is buying tests and Amber knows something about it, but she won't tell me because she's afraid of incriminating herself. She called it 'the amendment thing.' "

Crystal looked surprised and then she laughed. The laugh put Danny at ease. He smiled and continued his story, explaining that he could not go out with her again. "She's sweet on me, CJ, uh, Crystal. And I only went out with her because I knew she had some information. Honest." He raised his right hand like he was swearing a promise. "But I can't go out with her again. You know, she kissed me. Twice!"

Crystal turned and looked at him. She shook her head. "Ah, Danny. You get yourself into some of the weirdest messes." She paused a minute. "Hmm. Just what is it you want me to do? I already told you I am not helping you with what you call your first murder case. I told you to lay off that one. Captain Mitchell would be really mad if you were investigating Ms. Quinn's murder."

"This is different, CJ, Crystal."

"Good, Danny, you're starting to remember." She smiled.

"Crystal, this is about some kind of illegal activity going on in the Athletics Department. Coach Kelly is buying tests for the football players so they will remain eligible to play and I want you to find out from Amber how it works."

She was quiet as she drove the squad car around the gymnasium and out the back entrance. She took a deep breath and finally spoke.

"OK. I'll see what I can find out. But, I can't promise you anything."

Danny was so excited he reached out to hug her. She slapped his hands away and looked at him. "You're in too much trouble now, boy. Don't you think you better be on your way and try to straighten some of it out?"

Danny hopped out of the patrol car, then turned and waved at Crystal. She was smiling at him.

Chapter Nineteen

Jade Learns the Truth

JADE SAT UP perfectly straight on the cafeteria chair and stared across the table. She heard the words, but they seemed to be coming from far away.

"Hey, girl, you still with me?" Crystal asked again, sounding concerned.

Jade could hear Crystal's voice like it was speaking to her from the fog over the water. She shook herself awake and answered, "Yes. I'm here."

"So, what are you going to do about it?" Crystal asked.

"About what?" Jade's voice was soft.

"OK. Let's try this again." Crystal started to talk, but Jade put up her hand to stop her.

She spoke in a stronger voice, "No. Stop. I've got it. You're right. I'm the one to handle this situation." She paused before continuing, "I will." Her voice began to pick up volume and speed and she began to think out loud. She was perfectly calm as she started repeating the story that Crystal had just told her.

"OK. I want to be sure I've got this straight. Danny told you this. He said he went to the football game with Amber to pump her for information. He found out that Coach Kelly is buying tests for the players so they will pass their classes and still be able to play football. Right?"

Crystal only nodded and Jade continued.

"So Danny asked you to find out from Amber how this test stealing business works." She stopped again and Crystal nodded again. "And you think I should go talk to Amber instead because Amber is trying to steal Danny away from me." Jade pursed her lips and wrinkled her forehead.

"I'm on it," Jade said abruptly. She straightened her uniform, lifted her head high and tossed her long dark hair over her shoulder. She didn't even say good-bye, but left Crystal with her eyes wide and mouth hanging open. Jade marched out the door of the cafeteria like she was going to war. She walked fast and straight toward the Duplicating Office on the first floor of Peterson Hall. She felt her jaw get tight and she squinted her eyes.

The door of the Duplicating Office was open and there was a long line of teachers waiting to use the machines or pick up orders placed earlier. Jade walked around the bodies in line, ignoring them. She walked straight to the front counter and stood right in front of Amber, who was just finishing delivering an order to a teacher's assistant. Jade stood still and placed her hands flat on the counter. She looked up into Amber's face. She figured Amber was about three inches taller and thirty pounds heavier, but she had the power of anger on her side. She looked into Amber's face but could not tell what was there.

Amber spoke first, "There is a line. If you want help, you will have to wait your turn." Then she turned away to invite another person to the counter for help. Jade noticed that she did not call her by name. She thought Amber was trying to avoid this conversation as long as possible. She must know what it is about.

Jade lifted her hand like she was directing traffic. "Police business, Amber. I need to talk to you. Now." And she pointed her finger at Amber's chest.

She watched Amber turn her eyes down to hide whatever feeling was inside. Jade waited. Amber ignored her and said to the next person in line, "Mr. Taylor, may I help you?"

Jade had not noticed the math teacher in line but nodded at him and spoke, "Mr. Taylor, you will have to excuse us. I have some urgent police business with Amber and she will not be able to assist you right now." Then she looked at Amber and spoke again. "Call Tiffany or whoever is in charge today. You are coming with me."

Amber faced her defiantly. "I am not going anywhere with you. I'm working now."

Jade decided not to argue with her, but opened the swinging door that led behind the counter. She walked to the offices in back and poked her head in every doorway until she found somebody. It was Tiffany.

"Hey Tiffany. You're needed up front." Jade took a good look at Tiffany. She was wearing her black wool power suit with a red silk blouse. She was ready for business.

"Well, I'm sorry, but I'm busy right now, Jade. Can't it wait?"

Jade didn't hesitate. "No, it can't wait."

Tiffany looked at Jade's face, got up slowly and walked to the front counter. Jade followed two steps behind her. When they reached the counter, she stepped behind Amber and put her hand on Amber's shoulder as if they were long-time friends.

"Come with me, Amber."

Amber started to protest, but Jade grabbed her wrist and held it tightly. She pulled Amber out the door and into the hall, paying no attention to the crowd of people staring at the little police officer who looked like she was about to arrest a criminal.

Chapter Twenty

Confrontation

"WHAT ARE YOU doing? Let me go. I'm going to report you. This is police brutality!" Let go of me." Amber's voice was almost a squeak.

There was nobody in the hall, but Jade decided it would be safer to conduct this investigation in the little space beside the soda machine. They would not be visible to people passing by.

Jade looked down at the wrist she was holding and the snake that curled around the arm. She pushed Amber's body backward against the soda machine, and the machine clanged like a bell. Amber hit her head and yelped, "Ouch! Stop that! Let me go!"

Jade looked directly into Amber's eyes but did not let go of her wrist. She ignored the complaints. She was fired with anger and determination. She spoke calmly, but with steel in her voice. "I need some information, Amber, and you are the one who is going to give it to me."

"What are you talking about? I don't know anything! Let me go." But her voice was even weaker now.

Jade kept her voice low. "Oh, but I think you do know something. And you're going to tell me."

Amber closed her lips tightly like a child trying to keep a secret. She wouldn't look at Jade. She closed her eyes and put her finger-nail in her mouth and started biting it. Jade jerked lightly on Amber's wrist as she spoke. "Closing your eyes won't make me go away. And didn't your mother tell you not to bite your fingernails? Now. Tell me about the little scam you have going on there in the Duplicating Office. Who's in charge? How does it work? What is your part in it? Did Ms. Quinn know about this?" She hit her with questions like she wanted to hit her with fists. Then she waited.

Amber was silent for a long time. Jade waited. She knew the information was coming. Then, Amber opened her eyes and Jade could see tears forming in the corners. Amber was afraid of her! Jade didn't give in. She decided to ask one question and wait for the answer. "Who's in charge?"

Now the tears were rolling down Amber's plump cheeks. Her

makeup ran with the tears. She had blue and black stripes running from her eyes to her chin. She finally opened her mouth. "Tiffany."

Jade was surprised, but didn't want to show it. Of course, that is why Tiffany always looked so well dressed. She had extra money coming in. Nice little business. Jade asked her next question, "How does it work?"

Amber started slowly. "Well, the coach, he comes in here and talks with Tiffany. He tells her what he needs." As she talked, she warmed up a little and started talking faster, with more enthusiasm. "And then Tiffany says which tests she wants pulled out. The coach pays her. . ."

Jade interrupted her. "And what is your part in this business?"

Amber hesitated. "Well, I'm new. I just make the copies. Whatever she tells me to make. Honest. She gives me a little slip of paper with initials and the number of copies I need to make."

Jade tightened her grip on Amber's wrist. "You get paid, too, don't you? That's why you're driving that new little red car I saw you in the other night at the football game." She looked at Amber's face for a reaction. She didn't see one.

Jade spoke again. "How much do they pay you for your part in this little deal?" Amber kept her mouth closed and her eyelids lowered. She didn't look like she was going to answer. Jade figured this wasn't the most important piece of information, so she didn't push.

"How often does the coach come in here with these orders?"

Amber answered right away. "About three, maybe four times a month."

Jade had another question to ask her. "Do the teachers know anything about this?"

"No, uh, no," Amber replied and shook her head a little too hard. Jade didn't believe her.

"Who knows about this, Amber?" Jade's voice was tough as steel.

The tears formed again in Amber's eyes and she wouldn't or couldn't speak. Jade waited. Amber leaned her head back against the soda machine and it clanged again. She tried to wipe her wet face on the sleeve of her shirt. Jade let go of the wrist she was holding. She didn't think Amber was going to run anywhere.

Jade asked again in a softer voice. "Who knows about this? Which of the teachers?"

Amber's eyes were on the floor and her voice was very soft again. "Nobody." Then she raised her eyes from the floor and looked at Jade. "Nobody now."

Jade was puzzled. She was thinking. Ms. Quinn? Did she know? Is that why she was killed? She asked Amber, whose face was completely wet now.

"I think she found out." She used the sleeve of her shirt again to wipe her face. There were black and blue stripes running down her right sleeve. She started to walk away. Jade grabbed Amber's shirt-tail and pulled her back.

"There is one more thing, Amber."

Amber looked at Jade with a questioning expression. Quickly and without warning, Jade grabbed Amber's wrist with the tattoo and twisted her arm behind her back. Amber squeaked again. Jade put her mouth to Amber's ear and almost whispered this time. She spoke slowly and deliberately, but quite calmly. "If you ever get near Danny again, this snake is going to bite you in the backside." She released the wrist abruptly and walked out of the building, head held high. She passed the old Vietnamese janitor, who must have just come in. His head moved back and forth from Amber to Jade and back again. Jade smiled at him and kept on walking.

Chapter Twenty-one

Mr. Taylor's Office

AT 1:00 ON Monday afternoon, Danny took the steps of Peterson Hall two at a time from the fifth to the seventh floor. He didn't want to be late for Mr. Taylor's office hours. He really didn't know what to expect, but he felt that it was necessary to talk with the math teacher. Maybe he knew something about how this test stealing worked. Amber said lots of people had seen Mr. Taylor's math test. Maybe he was even part of it.

After he passed through the heavy outer doors, Danny had to walk past Ms. Quinn's office on his way to see the math teacher. He noticed the yellow tape across the door. He wanted to walk over to her door and poke his head inside, but he knew he shouldn't do that. He continued down the hall.

When Danny arrived at Mr. Taylor's office, there was another student already ahead of him. Danny stood outside in the hall and looked at the card on the office door. Professor Harvey Taylor. Mathematics. There was also information on the times and locations of the classes he was teaching this semester, and the required office hours. "Harvey" he repeated under his breath. "Ruby and Harvey?" He shook his head and shrugged.

In just a few minutes, a short blond guy, who looked about 15 years old but had to be older, came out the door. Danny didn't know him, but nodded as the other student passed by. The student looked at Danny and whispered under his breath, "The guy is nuts!" He kept on walking toward the door, shaking his head, obviously upset about something.

Danny poked his head in the open door and at the same time, tapped lightly with his knuckles to let the teacher know that he had a visitor. Harvey Taylor was seated at his desk doing nothing. He was staring into space, not seeing or hearing anything around him, apparently. Danny knocked again, this time louder. He cleared his throat and called out to him, "Mr. Taylor. Could I talk to you for a couple of minutes?"

The teacher jerked his head around quickly as if he were being pulled back from somewhere far away. He looked at Danny and waved him inside. He didn't smile.

Danny stood beside the desk and searched his mind for what he could say. He glanced around the room quickly and noticed the open window. He looked outside briefly and saw that they were above the teachers' parking lot. Not a very interesting view.

"Well, uh, I was wondering if, if you could help me." Without being asked, Danny sat down in the empty chair, which was facing the open window. He could see pigeons out on the ledge. He wondered absently if they ever got inside. Then he remembered that he wasn't here to think about pigeons. He had a job to do. He looked at the teacher.

"What can I help you with? Anything in particular?" Danny thought the voice sounded cold and emotionless, even though the words were neutral.

"Well," Danny stammered. "Well, I was wondering if you could help me with my math."

"That's my job. What in particular are you having trouble with?" Mr. Taylor looked directly at him.

Danny scolded himself silently. Damn! I didn't bring my book. I didn't decide what my problem was going to be. I am not prepared for this interview. But he didn't say any of this. Instead, he asked if he could look at the textbook they were using in the class.

Mr. Taylor reached above his head, pulled down the textbook and handed it to Danny without speaking. Danny opened the book and fumbled, turning pages back and forth until he came to a page he recognized. It was a recent lesson. He looked more carefully at the page and then pointed to a problem near the bottom.

The teacher looked at the open book, then at Danny and spoke in his familiar slow monotone, "Mr. Soto, you always do the operations in the parentheses first. Then exponents. Then multiplication, division, addition, and subtraction. In that order." He took the book back from Danny and waited for him to ask more questions.

Since he couldn't think of anything else to ask, he smiled and said, "Thanks. Let me think about that." Then he remembered the test.

"Oh, when did you say we would have the test? Next week?" He was stalling and was pretty sure Mr. Taylor knew it.

"Yes. Next week."

Danny decided he had completely wasted his time this afternoon. He had found out nothing. His eyes scanned the room. He couldn't see anything unusual, so he started to rise from his chair. As he stood, he noticed a small spider running across the top of the desk. Without a word, Mr. Taylor dropped the heavy textbook on the desk. It made a thumping noise. Danny jumped just a little, but watched his teacher pick up the book, reach for a tissue and wipe off the dead spider that was smashed partly on the desk and partly on the book.

Danny looked at him, but Mr. Taylor said nothing. He replaced the textbook on the bookshelf and turned back to Danny. "Anything else?"

Danny shook his head and rose from his chair. He thanked Mr. Taylor for his time and left the office. He was shaking his head and talking to himself as he walked down the stairs. "That guy is weird."

Chapter Twenty-two

Danny Talks to the Coach

CRIMINAL JUSTICE class 101 was almost over for today. Danny sat listening intently to Captain Mitchell drone on about interrogating witnesses.

"They will ask you questions. Avoid answering them. Deflect the questions. You will not want the witness to have ammunition against you, the crime, or the criminal. When they ask you—and they will—why you are questioning them, simply say that it is routine. You are questioning several people. You are just trying to piece the story together. Give out no more information than that. And one more thing: Always be prepared for the interview."

The bell rang and Captain Mitchell dismissed the class.

Danny sat there for a minute longer thinking about how this lecture might help him with his most immediate problem. He needed to talk with Coach Kelly and he hoped he would be prepared. He hoped that he wouldn't make any of the mistakes he made earlier today when trying to interview Mr. Taylor. Danny shook his head now remembering those mistakes.

He checked his watch. 2:30. He knew that football practice began at 3:15. Should he try to catch him before or after football practice? When would he have the advantage? He should probably take him by surprise, off guard, while he was fresh. Now, before football practice would be better. He wondered how to approach this so that the coach would not be suspicious. Then he stood up, straightened out his uniform and walked swiftly toward the gymnasium.

When he arrived at the gym, he saw the coach's office door open about halfway. He looked in to see Coach Kelly sitting at his desk, his feet propped up on the desk. He was reading the newspaper. It looked like the sports section. Danny knocked lightly on the door to get the coach's attention.

"Hey, Coach," Danny said brightly and flashed a smile.

"Danny boy," the coach smiled back and put down the paper, "this is a surprise. What's up?"

"Just thought I'd stop by and chat. You know I really miss playing football."

"I know you do. You've got talent, my boy. Hate to see that go to waste."

"I was just wondering. Is it too late? It's really just the beginning of the season."

"Yeah, but these guys have been in training for several months. It wouldn't be fair to let you join the team now."

This wasn't going the way he had planned, so Danny tried to think quickly. He thought of another idea.

"Well, what about for the next semester? I was thinking I want to play again before I graduate. You know, I've been going to school part-time, so it's taking me longer than two years."

"When do you graduate?"

"Probably in two semesters. But I'm really not sure. Anyway, Coach, I was wondering if you could help me out. I always have some trouble keeping my grades up when I play sports, so I was wondering if you might be able to help me."

Coach Kelly looked a little surprised and Danny thought he saw just a flicker of fear in his eyes.

"How do you mean that? You know that you have to keep up your grades or you get kicked off the team. Asked to leave. It's the law now. And, I have to say, I agree with it. I think all sportsmen should get a good academic education along with learning expertise in sports. It's just good financial planning."

Danny thought that sounded logical, but it didn't fit with what Amber had told him about the coach buying tests from the duplicating office. Coach Kelly was not going to give anything away. The police uniform probably didn't make the coach feel comfortable. That was another mistake Danny thought, coming in uniform, but he was here now and did not want to give up on the questioning.

"What I mean is, could you recommend a tutor in math or maybe a team study group so that I could feel more comfortable, more assured that I would pass my classes. Could you?"

Coach Kelly blinked and Danny wondered if the coach felt just a little bit relieved that Danny wasn't going to ask him about anything more than tutors. The coach relaxed his face muscles.

"Well, now that you mention it, maybe I could find someone who could tutor you. I'm not sure what they charge, but I'll look into it."

Danny gave him an over-bright smile. "Thanks, Coach. You know I've been wondering how all these guys do it. I don't think they're any smarter than me. I figured there was some way of getting help."

He saw the coach's face muscles tighten up. Ah, he's nervous. Looks like he's hiding something. Danny stood up, ready to leave. "Thanks again, Coach. Why don't I come back in a couple of days?

Maybe you'll have some information by then."

Danny gave the coach a quick wave of the hand and he was off, looking innocent, he hoped.

Chapter Twenty-three

Monday Afternoon Meeting

THERE WAS A regular meeting on Monday afternoons for student police officers and everyone in the department was required to attend. Danny arrived at the meeting a couple of minutes late. He sat at one of the few empty desks near the back of the room and against the wall. He leaned his head against the wall and looked around at the full room. Captain Mitchell was talking and Danny tried to listen, but was distracted. He could see the back of Jade's head. He recognized her long black hair that was coming loose from under her police cap. She was sitting near the front with Crystal, and they probably didn't even know he was there. He sighed and rubbed his hands over his face.

Captain Mitchell talked on. "And another thing. There have been several reports of theft and vandalism in the parking lots, especially during sports events. There were a couple of broken car windows last Friday night at the football game. There were also reports of stolen CD and tape players. Now, I forget. Who was working last Friday night?"

Jade was attending the meeting in body only. Her mind was still with Amber. She remembered questions that she should have asked but didn't. She was also trying to figure out how to tell Captain Mitchell. Or, she thought, maybe she didn't have to. Maybe Amber would turn herself in. Then again, probably not. It would be up to Jade to tell Captain Mitchell. But how? Her head hurt. She would figure this out. She just couldn't do it right now. Suddenly, she felt a poke in her ribs. She turned to look at Crystal. Crystal poked her again and started to speak.

"Captain Mitchell, I was actually scheduled to work, but traded with Officer Lee. She worked last Friday night."

Jade drew her attention back immediately. "Yes, sir. I was on duty Friday night."

Captain Mitchell asked, "Well, did you see anything unusual during the game while you were on duty?"

She wanted to say, "Yes, I saw my boyfriend out with another girl. And she kissed him." But she held her tongue and thought a minute. Oh, yes! The parking lot, the flashlight, the car roaring away!

"Actually, Captain, I did. Sorry I didn't report it. It was late and with the weekend in between I completely forgot."

The police captain looked at her strangely for a minute. Then he spoke. "What happened?" he asked rather sharply.

Jade wet her lips with her tongue before she started to speak. "Well, it was near the end of the game and I was making rounds. I didn't see anything until I got to about," she paused for a minute, "hmm, aisle five. I heard a noise and saw a flashlight. I went to investigate, but whoever it was flashed the light right in my eyes and I couldn't see. They got away." She paused again before continuing. "I did hear one of them calling to the other. He called him 'Tom.' "

Danny, sitting in the back, had closed his eyes for a minute, but opened them again when he heard Jade's voice. He hadn't talked to her in several days. He was wondering if he would ever hear her voice again. She always spoke so softly. He started to lean forward because he didn't want to miss one word! He leaned forward, straining to hear until the student desk he was sitting in crashed to the floor.

Every head in the room turned to see what had made such a noise. Jade turned with the others and found herself staring straight into Danny's eyes. She watched as his face grew bright red.

Danny tore his eyes away from Jade and got up from the floor. He picked up the desk and set it upright again before he sat down. He could hear laughter from several places in the room, but he tried to ignore it.

At the front of the room, Captain Mitchell looked at the red-faced student, too. "Soto, are you OK?" he asked.

"Yes," Danny's voice came out in a near whisper. He cleared his throat and spoke louder. "Sorry, Captain. You know how unsteady these desks are."

"Yes. Now, as you were saying, Officer Lee," and he turned his attention back to Jade, who finished her story quickly and then was quiet She tried to listen as the captain returned to his notes and mentioned several other matters that were important to the student police force.

The Chancellor reported that someone had parked in his reserved parking space three times last week. Officers on duty in the morning must now put orange plastic cones in that space to stop students and teachers from parking in the Chancellor's parking space. Also the cafeteria reported twenty sets of silverware missing in one day last week. The cooking school thinks it might be the football team. Any officers who happen to be in the cafeteria should keep their eyes open and report any theft.

"But, remember," he said, "you can only. . ."

The entire group of students interrupted him together like a chorus, "direct traffic, write tickets and respond to emergencies," they finished his sentence and laughter broke out in the room.

The captain didn't laugh, but said, "I'm glad you know something about your job."

When the meeting was ready to break up, one of the students raised a hand and asked the captain a question. "What is happening with Ms. Quinn's murder investigation?"

The captain raised his voice to be heard above the sliding chairs and general confusion as some students prepared to leave. "There is no new information on the murder. But I want to remind you that as student police officers, you are not allowed to participate in this investigation."

Students began to walk out of the room, but Captain Mitchell spoke again. "I would like to see officers Soto, Lee and Jackson, please. Right now."

Crystal and Jade turned to look at each other and remained seated.

Chapter Twenty-four

Suspended

HEARING HIS name, Danny started to the front of the room, but hesitated when he wasn't sure where to sit. He picked the chair on the other side of Jade, but before he could sit down, he felt a tug on his sleeve and looked down at Crystal who pointed to the seat right beside her. He decided she was probably right and moved to the desk beside Crystal. He knew that this was not the right place for him to try to talk to Jade. Maybe he could catch her after they listened to whatever the captain had to tell them.

Captain Mitchell remained standing. He looked like a stern father about to punish his children. He cleared his throat and looked directly at Jade. "Officer Lee, you have violated at least two of the regulations for student officers here at Ocean View College. I am sure you know what they are. You did not report the incident in the parking lot Friday night. It is regulation that any such disturbance be reported within 24 hours. If you were not able to file a written report, you should have called in the report the next morning at least. I know that would have been Saturday, but we do have an answering machine and a FAX machine. You could have called me on my cell phone, too. You were negligent in your duties." He stopped talking. Jade's face began to turn red and she lowered her head. She looked disappointed in herself.

"And that's not all," the captain continued his speech. Jade raised her head to look at the captain. "I received a report earlier that you attacked a student worker in Peterson Hall this morning. The student claims that you embarrassed her in front of her colleagues and other students and that you hurt her physically. This conduct is unbecoming to an officer of the law. And you know that. You will be suspended for an appropriate period of time."

Captain Mitchell paused before continuing his speech. "Now, do you have anything to say in your own defense?" He waited for her to respond.

"I plead guilty to the first charge. And I apologize. I was negligent. But, the second charge is . . ." she took a deep breath.

The captain scratched his bald head and looked at her. "I'm listening," he said.

"The second charge is false, I mean it was justified. I mean. . ." She stopped and started again. "Captain Mitchell, I heard about a scheme operating out of the duplicating office. A group of students steals, copies and sells tests to the football coach. The coach buys them so that his players can pass their academic courses and continue to play football."

Captain Mitchell wrinkled up his face. "Is this true? How did you find out about it?"

"Yes, sir. It wasn't easy, but I got the information out of Amber Jones. She's the one who filed the complaint against me, I'm sure."

"Good work, Officer Lee, but you're still suspended."

She started to argue with him, but his face said, "Don't argue. You can't win."

Danny sat quietly beside Crystal, attentive while the captain scolded Jade. But he knew he could not let Jade take the blame for something he had started.

"Captain Mitchell," Danny drew the captain's attention in his direction. "I would like to explain that I had a part in this and it was actually my fault. I heard about this duplicating scam but did not get all of the necessary information and I asked Jade, uh, Officer Lee, to interrogate the witness. You see, she's a girl, and I was in the position, you see. I'm a guy, and she—the other girl, Amber—is a girl. And she thought I liked her or something. So I asked another officer to interrogate Amber."

"I see. You asked Officer Lee to interrogate Amber Jones."

Just then, Crystal spoke up. "Captain Mitchell, actually, Danny told me about what he suspected and asked me to interrogate Amber. I suggested that Jade should do the questioning."

The captain turned his attention to Crystal and Danny. "This is all very confusing. Anyway, I wanted to talk to you two because you, Jackson, are the unit leader, and you, Soto, have been in charge of going to classes and asking for information regarding witnesses to the murder last week. And of course, that is the only part of this murder investigation that you are allowed to participate in." He looked sternly at Danny. "But now. . ." He didn't finish the sentence.

The three students watched Captain Mitchell shake his head and look at each of them in turn. He twisted his mouth into a frown. "But, if all of you are actually to blame for this incident," he said, "then, you're all suspended."

The three students sat there for a minute in surprise. They didn't know what to say, but were afraid to argue, especially since the captain didn't seem to be in a really good mood. Then Danny spoke, "Captain Mitchell, I haven't been very successful with my job. I have visited a few classes, but nobody admits seeing anything. I have a question for you."

"Go ahead." The captain looked directly at Danny.

"Do you think that Ms. Quinn knew about this duplicating scheme? Do you think maybe that's what got her killed?"

The captain was thoughtful for a minute then he answered in a low voice. "Could be. Maybe she found out." He turned his head and stared as if he were far away. Then he started talking again, but this time he was mumbling to himself. "She always kept in touch with the coach, even after they broke off their engagement. They were friendly. She could have found out."

Danny, Jade and Crystal sat watching intently and leaned forward in their chairs to catch every word. They saw a quick look of surprise on his face when he turned back and saw them sitting there. The captain must have forgotten where he was. "I would like to remind you that you are all suspended. No more class visits. No more interrogations. Leave it to the police. You three are relieved of your duties for a week. While you are on suspension, report in to me daily. Understand?"

"Yes, sir," the three students answered in unison and nodded. They watched Captain Mitchell walk out of the room.

Chapter Twenty-five

Tackle

WHEN THE DOOR closed behind Captain Mitchell, the three students took a deep breath all together. Danny turned toward Jade with a pleading expression. He didn't even open his mouth to speak before Jade said, "Just leave me alone," in a voice edged with steel. He looked down at the desk but did not get up to leave. He decided to speak to Crystal.

"CJ," he said and she looked at him sternly. "I mean Crystal," he corrected himself. He did not continue, though, because she was speaking to him.

"Danny Soto. You are mostly responsible for our suspensions and this whole mess. I do not want to see or talk to you right now. Give me some time." With these words, she stood abruptly and walked out of the room. Jade stood too and marched right behind her friend without even looking at Danny. She thought he needed to suffer just a little more.

Danny sat alone in the police meeting room and thought. Yes, it really was his fault that they had all been suspended. And if he had not gone out with Amber, Jade would not be mad at him. And if he had not dragged Crystal into it by asking for her help. . . He couldn't finish the thought because there was something troubling him. Something the captain said. What was it? He stood up and began to pace the room, his usual thinking pose. He went up and down the middle aisle of the room trying to remember just what it was that bothered him.

That was it! The captain said that Coach Kelly and Ruby Quinn were engaged at one time. Did the captain really say this, or was Danny imagining it? Do you suppose. . . ? No. The coach wouldn't do that. Or would he? Do you suppose that he could have killed her? Maybe he still loved her. Maybe he was jealous that she was going to marry old man Taylor—Harvey. Well, he has to be a shady guy. He proved that by buying those tests. But, could he actually kill someone?

He stopped in mid-pace and slammed his right fist into his open left hand. "There's only one way to find out!" he said to the empty room. He ran out the door and down the hill to the gymnasium. If he got lucky, he could catch the coach just before he left for the day. Danny stopped running when he reached the football field. He saw the coach standing alone near the goal posts at the opposite end. He was holding his clipboard and seemed to be reading something written there.

Danny walked as calmly as possible toward Coach Kelly, but was surprised when the coach looked up, saw Danny, threw the clipboard aside, and started to run just as Danny got near enough to speak. For a minute, Danny was confused, but his football instincts took over and he began to chase him. It looked like the coach was heading for the opposite goal posts. Danny wondered what was wrong with him, but didn't stop to think about it.

The coach looked back at Danny and kept on running. Danny shouted at the coach, "Stop! I need to talk to you." The coach didn't stop. Danny turned up the heat and at the 10-yard line just before they reached the goal, Danny grabbed him around the waist and pulled him to the ground in a perfect tackle.

"Damn it! Get off! Get off me!" the coach shouted. "Let me go!"

They were both out of breath when they stood up, but Danny was younger and in better shape. The coach was bent over at the waist, breathing hard. Danny grabbed the sleeve of the coach's jacket and tugged. "I need to talk to you."

The coach straightened up and held up both hands in the air as if in surrender. "OK. OK, They told me that you knew. I guess you figured it out," he said. "I give up. I just did it because I couldn't see any other way."

"What do you mean you couldn't see any other way? Go on."

"We were winning, but we would have been in trouble if some of these guys had to be kicked off the team."

Danny realized that the coach was talking about the test scam and not about Ms. Quinn's murder. He wanted the coach to continue talking, just in case there was any new information. There wasn't.

"Amber?" Danny asked. "Did she warn you that you're going to get busted?"

The coach nodded.

After thinking a minute, Danny asked, "By any chance, Coach, did Ms. Quinn know anything about this test-buying deal? "

The coach put a hand over his eyes and said, "Oh, God."

Danny waited for him to continue. The coach seemed to be stuck, so Danny prodded him, "Did she?"

"Yeah. She found out. I didn't tell her, but somehow she found out. I tried to talk to her and explain, but she wanted to report it. We were trying to work out a deal when she got killed."

"Is that why she was killed?" Danny asked.

"Hey, man, I didn't kill her if that's what you're thinking. I liked Ruby."

"Weren't you engaged to her at one time?" Danny continued with his questions.

"Yes, but so what? We were friends. You know, Danny, this is none of your business."

The coach stepped away like he was ready to leave.

Danny grabbed his sleeve again. "Maybe you were a little jealous that she was about to marry someone else."

"Hell, no." The coach jerked his arm away and glared at Danny, "And I have had enough of this! Go ask her fiancé. Maybe he knows something."

He turned and walked away. Danny stood alone in the end zone.

Chapter Twenty-six

Another Plan

AFTER DANNY watched the coach disappear into the gymnasium, he turned and started walking back toward the police bungalow. Then it hit him. He was supposed to be on suspension, which meant that he did not have any student police duties like directing traffic in the morning or writing parking tickets for cars parked in the chancellor's reserved space or any other illegally parked cars. That meant he didn't have to get up early. It also meant that his interrogation of Coach Kelly might have been a very big mistake. But, who was going to tell Captain Mitchell? Certainly not the guilty coach. He relaxed, believing he was safe for a while.

As his long legs carried him back up the hill, Danny was thinking. The coach said Ms. Quinn knew about the test-buying scheme. He also said that he didn't kill her. But, of course, they always say that whether they are guilty or not. So, claiming he was innocent didn't actually make him innocent. But, then again, what did he say about Mr. Taylor? "Ask her fiancé," or something like that. Anyway, what would he ask Mr. Taylor? "Did you kill Ruby Quinn?" Stupid question. Everybody answers no to that question. Danny rolled his head from side to side to ease some tension.

By the time he was near the police bungalow, a plan began to form in his mind. He would just pay a little visit to Captain Mitchell in the police bungalow. The captain didn't tell him to stay away from the bungalow, just that he didn't have any police duties. In fact, the captain had told him to check in once a day. He would start right now.

The visit to the math teacher's office that afternoon had given him no information. Nothing, except now he didn't just think Mr. Taylor was weird; he was sure of it. Maybe the way to get information was to go at night, late, after everyone was gone. But what would he be looking for? He didn't know, but it sounded exciting, and since he couldn't do anything that Captain Mitchell would hear about, he thought a midnight visit to Mr. Taylor's office might turn up something. Police investigators just never know what they will find. All he needed was the master key to the offices in Peterson

Hall. And he knew where he could find it.

When he reached the door of the police bungalow, Danny decided that the first thing he should do is "check in" as Captain Mitchell instructed them all to do once a day.

Captain Mitchell was behind the counter, shuffling papers. They looked like parking tickets. He examined each one and then counted the stack and bundled them with a rubber band. Danny cleared his throat to get the captain's attention.

When the captain looked up, Danny said, "Captain Mitchell, I'm just checking in like you asked us to."

The captain scratched his bald head with his thick fingers before he spoke, "Isn't this a little soon? You were just suspended about an hour ago. You can wait until tomorrow to check in, Soto." He returned immediately to another stack of paper work in front of him.

Danny replied, "Well, sir, I just wanted to get started off on the right foot. I've never been suspended before. Does this go on my record?"

"Yes," the captain answered, "and it affects your grade."

"I thought it probably worked like that." He pointed to the water cooler and continued, "I'd just like a drink of water, sir, before I leave for the day. OK?"

"Help yourself," the captain replied without even looking up this time.

Danny stepped to the back of the office where the water cooler sat in a stand near the window. The water cooler was also near the key rack. He figured this part would be easy, as easy as a drink of water. He walked calmly toward the cooler, took a paper cup from the cup holder and filled it. Then he turned slowly as he drank so that he could keep an eye on the captain. He held the paper cup in one hand and sipped the cool water slowly. Quickly, he moved his eyes toward the keys, trying to spot the right one. There it was at the end of the row. He turned his back toward the captain to hide his movements and pretended to be looking at the old photographs of earlier campus police captains on the wall at the back.

Danny lifted the master key quietly and closed his fist around it, then casually, put his hand in his pants pocket. He figured he would bring it back before anyone missed it. They only used these master keys in case of emergency—like murder—and he sure hoped there wouldn't ever be another murder at Ocean View College.

He turned slowly to look at the captain who still looked busy. He was operating a calculator now.

Danny drank the last of his water and tossed the paper cup in the wastebasket. He headed for the door. On the way out, he spoke to Captain Mitchell.

"So long, Captain. I'll check in tomorrow."

Chapter Twenty-seven

Midnight Adventure

ON THE WAY out the door, Danny's heart was pounding wildly. Since he was already on suspension, he thought he might as well break some more rules. He had just stolen a key and he had plans for some real detective work tonight. He was already receiving the punishment, so he might as well get the most out of it. As he drove home in his old white Ford Mustang, he was planning for his midnight adventure.

Midnight, or maybe 12:30, he figured was the best time. By then, all of the teachers and students would be gone. The library would be locked up and he believed the night janitors would be on their lunch break. Yes, that was the best time.

At dinner, Danny was unusually quiet. He was afraid and ashamed to tell his parents about the suspension. His father was so proud that Danny was in the police training program and would be angry and disappointed to hear that Danny had broken rules and Captain Mitchell had placed him on suspension. There wasn't much else for him to talk about, so he kept his mouth shut. The rest of his siblings made up for him, though, and jabbered on and on about one thing and another. Danny barely paid attention. His mind was on this his plans for later that night.

After dinner and household chores, Danny went to his room with the excuse that he needed to study for exams coming up next week, which wasn't exactly a lie. Actually, he lay flat on his back on the bed and stared at the ceiling. Then he decided to close his eyes and try to rest just a little before he had to go. Without planning to, he fell asleep.

He woke up when he heard a toilet flush upstairs. It must have been one of his brothers who slept upstairs. He was a little confused at first. He looked down the length of his body. He was completely dressed. He still had his shoes on! What happened? Then he remembered. Damn! He looked at his watch. It was 12:05. He could still make it while the janitors were on their break. He listened hard to hear if his brother was still awake. No noise. Good. He picked up his jacket that was on the back of the desk chair. He picked up the police issue flashlight from the desk where he always kept it handy. He hung it on the strap on his belt.

Danny tiptoed to the door and carefully turned the knob. The floorboards in front of his bedroom door squeaked. He stopped and listened again. He heard nothing. He slipped out the back door and into the Mustang. He warmed up the engine and drove back to school.

When he arrived at the campus, he parked behind Peterson Hal in the teachers' parking lot, hidden from view just in case the regular campus police happened to pass by and wonder why this car was there at this time of night. He still had the master key in his pocket. He reached his hand in his pocket and felt the key just to be sure. The master key for Peterson Hall opened all the doors in the building, including the outer doors. He would also need the flashlight. He patted his side to make sure the flashlight was still there.

When he got to the back door, he looked around in all directions. He couldn't see or hear anyone. He slipped the key from his pocket and inserted it into the keyhole. The door opened immediately. He decided to leave it open in case he needed to make a fast getaway.

Once inside the building, it seemed like it was going to be easy. In each hallway, there was one light on, but the stairway was not lit. Danny thought using the elevator might draw unwanted attention, so he climbed the stairs quickly and quietly to the seventh floor. When he got to the top, he found another locked door. This one, too, opened easily with the key. He went inside and walked past Ms. Quinn's office. He noticed that the yellow crime tape was still in place. He flashed the light on it. One corner of the tape was drooping. It looked like someone had removed it and then put it back up again. It was the city cops, most likely, while they were investigating.

He continued down the hall to Mr. Taylor's office. Mr. Taylor and Ms. Quinn had offices on the same floor, but on opposite ends of the hallway. When he reached the door of Mr. Taylor's office, he stopped again and looked around him. He shone his flashlight in all directions. He turned it off and listened. Nothing. He took the key from his pocket and inserted it into the lock. This door, too, opened right away. As he stepped inside, he wondered just what he was looking for. He stopped just in the doorway and thought for a second. He didn't know what it was, but he was hoping there was something here, something that would indicate who killed Ruby Quinn. How could he ever hope to find something when he didn't know what he wanted to find? He shrugged. He was already here now, so he might as well look around.

He turned on the flashlight again and shone the light around the small office to get a sense of the room and where he might start looking. Then he walked over to the window and looked at the ledge and the parking lot below. He could see his car and two others in the lot behind the building. Had there been three cars in the parking lot when he parked? He couldn't remember. Janitors, probably, but he knew he needed to be careful. Maybe somebody else was around tonight. He turned back to the room and began to search from ceiling to floor. When the light reached the bookcase, he started his inspection on the top shelf. He noticed a layer of dust there around the books. Some of these books looked like they had never been opened. He read the titles printed on the spines: Elementary Math; Geometry; Algebra; Algebra Made Easy; College Math. He was careful not to touch or disturb anything.

He studied the structure of the bookcase. It was not solid, but open on the ends. The books were held on the shelves with heavy bookends in the shape of lion heads. He noticed that the dust on the back of the lower shelf had been disturbed. It was a long clean area about the size of a finger or a pencil. He flashed the light behind the books. There was something there. He could barely see it. It looked like the eraser end of a pencil. He reached for it, but remembered in time that he shouldn't touch anything. He didn't have any plastic gloves with him. Damn! How could he have forgotten to bring the plastic gloves? He shone the light around the office, looking for a tissue or a plastic bag, or a piece of cloth that he could use to pick up the object. The flashlight landed on a box of tissues on the desk, but as he reached for one, he thought he heard a noise. It sounded like the hallway door opening. Quickly, he switched off the light and pulled the office door almost closed. He moved deeper into the office and stood absolutely still.

He heard footsteps coming down the hall. They were coming toward him.

Chapter Twenty-eight

More Investigation

DANNY STOOD in the dark trying not to breathe too loudly, but his heart was pounding fast and hard. He was sure that the intruder could hear it. As the footsteps got nearer, he tried to think where he could hide or what excuse he would use if the janitors caught him here where he wasn't supposed to be.

The sound of the footsteps stopped right outside Mr. Taylor's office. Danny stood frozen to the spot. The door opened. By now Danny's eyes were adjusting to the darkness and he could see a person's head pop into view in the doorway. Was it? Could it possibly be? It was. He reached out his hand and grabbed the arm of the intruder. She started to scream and Danny covered her mouth with his hand.

"Shh!" he said and took his hand away from her mouth. He turned the flashlight on and shone the light up and down his partner.

"What are you doing here?" he asked Jade very softly.

"I came to ask you the same question," she whispered back.

"How did you know I was here?" he continued.

"I parked right beside you behind Peterson Hall."

"So that's your car out there. I didn't recognize it in the dark. That still doesn't answer my question, though. What are you doing on campus after midnight?" he asked.

"Probably the same thing you are. I'm suspended, too, you know and I also heard Captain Mitchell when he was talking to himself. He said that the coach used to be engaged to Ms. Quinn. I was going to go to the gymnasium and snoop around the coach's office, but I couldn't get in."

"How did you get in here?" he wanted to know.

"You left the door open, Danny."

"Oh, right. I did. But how were you planning to get in here without a key?"

"Well," Jade confessed, "I went first to the police bungalow. I was going to borrow the master key. But I saw that someone beat me to it. Now I know who."

He gave her a hug and she didn't push her away.

"What are we looking for, Danny?" she asked.

They were both whispering.

"I honestly don't know, but just before you scared the wits out of me a minute ago, I think I found something." He took her hand and led her over to the bookcase. He flashed the light behind the last book on the lower shelf.

She started to reach for the object, but Danny pulled her hand back. "I was just looking for something to use to pick it up. I don't want to destroy any fingerprints."

"Right," Jade said and pulled out a pair of thin plastic gloves from her back pocket and put them on. Because her hands were smaller, it was easier for her to reach behind the books in that small space without disturbing anything.

She pulled out the object and held it up. Danny focused the light on it. They both looked intently. It was part of a pencil, broken about in half. It was the shiny blue kind of pencil that Coach Kelly always used. On the part that had been broken, there was bare wood and spots of red mixed with blue paint chips.

"Blood!" Jade whispered in a voice a little too loud. She lowered her voice and continued. "You know what this means, don't you? It has to be Mr. Taylor! How else would it be here? But why? Why did he kill her?"

Jade held the pencil carefully in her hands as they talked.

"Maybe jealousy. That pencil looks like it belongs to the coach. Mr. Taylor must have known about the coach and Ms. Quinn. You know, that they were involved before. Maybe he saw them together. She knew about the duplicating scam. We already know that. Old man Taylor probably saw the pencil in her office and went ballistic."

Danny stopped talking when he heard the outer door to the hallway open with a squeak. He turned off the flashlight and grabbed Jade by the hand. He whispered in her ear, "Out the window."

Jade nodded and they crept to the window. Together they pushed it outward, trying not to make any noise. They could hear the footsteps coming closer. It sounded like they were coming right toward them.

They eased open the window and Jade quickly stepped out on the twelve-inch ledge that circled the whole building. Danny followed her just as quickly. Carefully, they walked one step at a time until they were several offices away from the now open window of Mr. Taylor's office. They saw a light go on in the building, somewhere near the office they had just left. Then they heard a window slam shut.

Danny and Jade stood on the ledge outside. They held hands and each one silently prayed.

Chapter Twenty-nine

On the Ledge

JADE SQUEEZED Danny's hand and closed her eyes. Even though it was dark and she could not see the ground, she knew that if one of them slipped, it would be the end. She was breathing quickly now. She tried to calm herself.

Danny spoke first in a soft voice. "Do you really need those gloves anymore?"

"No, I should take them. . ." She didn't finish her sentence, but started to whisper excitedly, "Danny, I've lost the pencil. I had it in my hand. Oh, no! I must have dropped it getting out the window. We lost our evidence!"

"Just be calm," Danny said and put his arm around her. "There isn't really anything we can do about it immediately. I'm not going back into that office right now. But I do think we should try to get off this ledge." He paused for a second. "There must be another open window. Let's go slowly."

"All right," Jade said in a small voice while she took off her plastic gloves and put them back in her pocket. "Let's not be in any hurry. It's an awful long way down there, and I would miss you a lot if you fell."

"Really?" He got excited and almost forgot where he was. "You know, I never really got to explain to you. About. . . uh, about. . ."

"Go ahead, Danny, say it. Amber. Her name is Amber and you had a date with her and she kissed you and I saw it." Now she was getting excited. She moved her right foot unconsciously, but the foot found no place to land. For a second, her body wavered and she thought she was going to fall, but she pulled her foot back quickly to the safety of the ledge. She took in a deep breath and Danny hugged her tighter.

They huddled together on the ledge, afraid to move or breathe too heavily. After a minute, their heartbeats had slowed down and Danny decided to finish his confession.

"Yes. I went out with Amber but it was almost an accident. You see, I was trying to find out what she knew about the murder and she was hinting around that something was going on in the dupli-

cating office. I didn't know any other way to get the information."
He paused before continuing. "But I'm sorry. I really am."

He could feel her body relax and then he felt her arms reaching
up around his neck. She pulled his head down gently and kissed
him softly. He was forgiven.

"Amber never kissed me like that," he teased.

"She'd better not," Jade responded. She changed the subject
abruptly. "Danny, we have to get off this ledge. It's giving me the
creeps."

"OK. Let's just inch our way along here. Not too fast."

For the next fifteen or twenty minutes, the two student police
officers slowly made their way along the ledge of the seventh floor
of Peterson Hall. They passed several windows but none was open.
They were getting discouraged.

Then Jade, who was in the lead position, said, "I think we've
found something. This window seems to be open a couple of inches. Let's get inside. Do you think that person is gone? Was it the
janitor? Mr. Taylor? Someone else?"

Danny whispered, "Hold on just a minute. Listen. Can you hear
any noise? Do you see any lights?"

They were both quiet and strained to hear any noise from inside
the building. Nothing. Jade turned to Danny and said, "I don't hear
a thing. No lights, either. Whoever it was must have come and
gone. Let's take a chance. We have to get inside. It's cold out here
as well as scary."

"All right. Go to the other side of the window and we can try to
reach in and open it wider so that we can get in. Careful, now, not
too fast. Watch your balance."

She inched her way to the opposite end of the window. Danny
was on the north side and she was on the south. Each one reached
a hand inside and pulled the window outward, open. It was now
wide enough for Jade to slip inside. Danny whispered, "You go
first."

Carefully, slowly, Jade pushed herself feet first through the open
window. She could see a bookcase just to the side of the window,
and searched with the toe of her boot for a place to step. She
found one on the corner of the bookcase. It was a short hop from
there to the floor. Then she poked her head out the window to talk
to Danny.

"Your turn. Let's open this a little wider for you. I'll help you get
in."

Danny made the same trip, but it was easier because his legs
were longer.

The two of them stood in this office and looked around. When they saw the yellow tape across the door, they realized where they were—Ms. Quinn's office. And, it was still officially a crime scene. Jade grabbed Danny's hand and whispered, "This is where she was killed. We're back where it all started."

After a minute, Danny spoke quietly, "Since we're here, maybe we should have a look around."
Jade replied, "Why not? We've broken every other rule tonight."

Chapter Thirty

More Company

DANNY AND JADE stood quietly for a moment in the middle of Ms. Quinn's office. They were listening for any suspicious noise. They heard nothing. There was no light coming in through the open doorway with the yellow tape across the opening. They decided it was safe to continue the search for clues at the crime scene.

Danny took his flashlight off his belt and switched it on. He moved the light beam slowly around the walls of the office, over the filing cabinets, the bookcases, and the desk. Again, they really didn't know what they were looking for.

When they got to the end of the bookcase, Danny shone the light on the computer. He stared at it for a minute, then turned to Jade and spoke in a whisper. "Wasn't that computer turned on the day of the murder? I remember a screen saver. Fish, wasn't it?"

"Right," Jade said, "I think that's right. But, so what?"

"Somebody turned it off."

"Probably somebody from the main office. Save energy, you know." Jade said, logically.

"But what if there was something on there that the killer didn't want anyone to see?" Danny was getting excited again.

"Like what?"

"E-mail," Danny said immediately.

"Could be. Why don't we try to get into her e-mail account? It wouldn't hurt to try."

"Here," Danny said, handing her the flashlight. "You give me some light and I'll try it out."

Jade shone the light over the keyboard and screen while Danny put on Jade's plastic gloves. Danny turned on the machine and waited for it to boot up. In a minute, the menu appeared. There was no request for a password. He hoped they could also get into her e-mail account without a password.

They weren't so lucky. Over his shoulder, he asked Jade, "What do you think she would use as a password?"

"Precious." The word came from somewhere behind them. Startled, they turned around quickly to see Harvey Taylor pointing a gun at the two of them. Jade dropped the flashlight.

"Precious," Mr. Taylor repeated the word and continued. "She thought that was funny. Rubies are precious. Her name was Ruby."

Jade realized her mouth was hanging open. She closed it. She looked at Danny. He didn't look afraid, except for the slight shaking of his hands. She realized that Danny's guess about the murderer was correct, but how were they ever going to get out of this one? Maybe Danny could talk their way out. Or maybe they could distract him. There was only one of him and there were two of them. Maybe. . .

"Mr. Taylor." Danny sounded calm, "What's going on? What are you doing here?"

"I saw your car out back in the parking lot. I figured you must still be snooping around." Holding the gun steady, he reached into his pants pocket with his other hand. "And I found this on the floor of my office." He held up the broken pencil. "You know, janitors turn on the lights. They don't work by flashlight. You must have gone out the window. I couldn't find you."

Danny's hands were shaking harder. He clutched his shirt to keep his hands still. He concentrated, trying to think what he could say next. "But what are you doing here so late at night?"

"Business. I had some business to take care of. On Ruby's computer. You see, there was some e-mail on there that might have made me look suspicious. I had to get rid of it. There was something going on between her and the coach. She wouldn't tell me, but I knew. They were seeing each other. They were going to get back together again. I'm sure of it."

Danny nodded. It sounded to him like Harvey Taylor was trying to excuse his actions. He didn't know what to say, so he said nothing. He could sense Jade beside him, but did not take his eyes off Mr. Taylor. Danny's mind was racing wildly, trying to figure out how to get them out of this office and away from this crazy man who was pointing a gun at them.

"Come on," Harvey Taylor said. "Let's get out of here. This little accident shouldn't happen at school." He waved the gun toward the door.

Jade was also trying to think how they could disarm their attacker. She looked around the room, but couldn't see anything that she could reach or throw. Her heart was pounding fiercely.

"Hey! Pick up that flashlight." Mr. Taylor pointed to the flashlight Jade had dropped. "We're not going to leave any evidence around for the police to find. Let's get out of here. Right now." He waved the gun in the direction of the door again.

Jade kept her eyes on Mr. Taylor as she reached down in one

quick motion, picked up the flashlight, switched it on and aimed the light directly into his eyes, surprising him. He blinked in an automatic response to the light.

Immediately, Jade shouted, "Danny!"

It was just enough time. Danny did not hesitate. When the teacher closed his eyes, Danny leapt across the small room and grabbed Mr. Harvey Taylor around the waist and pulled him down to the floor in another perfect football tackle.

Chapter Thirty-one

Capture

DANNY WAS ON the floor struggling with his math teacher, trying to gain control of him and take the gun away. He felt legs kicking him and hands beating on his back. He tried to pin down the older man's hands, but Mr. Taylor was stronger than he looked.

Jade watched in agony, trying to think how she could help Danny. She stepped closer and watched every move as the two men struggled. She wanted to help and was looking for an opportunity. She saw Danny grab for the hand holding the gun. He tried to pin that arm down to the floor, but the other hand grabbed Danny by the hair and pulled him up again, away from the gun.

Jade moved to the other side of the two men as they rolled around on the floor. Again, Danny grabbed the gun hand and tried to pull the gun away. Jade saw her chance. Danny was breathing hard, but managed to push the hand with the gun flat onto the floor. Jade immediately put her right boot heel on Mr. Taylor's knuckles and stepped down hard. Harvey Taylor let go of the gun and screamed. Jade picked up the gun, stepped back and pointed the weapon directly at the older man, who was out of breath and still lying on the floor.

"It's over, Mr. Taylor. You're under arrest," she said in a steady voice.

Danny stood, then reached down, grabbed the math teacher by the front of his shirt and pulled him to a sitting position. "Stand up!" he ordered in a voice full of authority.

Harvey Taylor was panting from the struggle. He sat on the floor and refused to stand. "You can't arrest me." He took two quick breaths before he continued. "You're not police officers." He took two more deep breaths. "You know," more quick breaths, "you are probably in more trouble than I am."

"I wouldn't bet on that," she said, keeping the gun pointed straight at him. But she took a quick look at Danny's face. He returned the look. She could read his thought. He wanted to know what they were going to do now. Harvey Taylor was right. They couldn't arrest him, at least not as police officers. But they were darn sure not going to just let him go.

"Actually," Jade said, "we can arrest you." We are responding to an emergency." Then she directed her words at Danny. "Let's find something to tie him up with."

"Good idea," Danny said, and he looked around the room for anything that might work. His eyes stopped on the yellow crime tape on the door. He stepped to the door and tore down the several strands of tape.

"I know this won't hold for very long, but we won't need it for very long." Danny carried the strips of tape from the door over to where their prisoner was still sitting on the floor, looking angry. Danny started at the shoulders and wound the tape tightly, around and around the Harvey Taylor's body. His hands were immobile and his legs were taped together. He wasn't going anywhere.

"Here, Danny," Jade said as she handed the gun to him, "I'm going to make a phone call."

She used the telephone in Ms. Quinn's office and punched in the number for the city police department. She spoke calmly. "My name is Jade Lee and I am a student police officer at Ocean View College. My partner and I have just subdued a man who was trying to kill us."

She answered a few more questions then hung up. It was all over now except for the waiting. And she knew that they would have to explain why they were on campus after midnight. The truth, of course, was always best. She didn't want to think how mad Captain Mitchell would be.

Chapter Thirty-two

Everything Changes

DANNY WALKED into the cafeteria carrying a bundle in a paper bag. It was about the size of a book and he held it casually in his right hand. He saw Jade and Crystal at their favorite table in the corner of the noisy room. He lifted the package in his hand and used it to wave a greeting. He walked straight to them, put the package down and gave Jade a little kiss on the cheek.

"You guys made up?" Crystal asked raising her eyebrows.

"We're working on it," Danny said. "This is the best part of a fight, you know."

Jade wrinkled her nose and Danny took a seat beside her. "Where's your coffee?" Danny asked her.

"Well, after that night in Ms. Quinn's office, I thought it was a sign. Life is short. Time for me to make some changes. I'm giving up coffee."

Danny lowered his head and looked at her. "Really?" he asked. "And what are you drinking instead?"

"Orange juice for now, but if I get frustrated, I'm switching to beer."

Crystal and Danny laughed. The three sat silently for a minute before they all started to speak at once and laughed again.

Crystal started again, "For now, Harvey Taylor is in jail. Captain Mitchell told me that he confessed. It was jealousy all along. He saw Ms. Quinn talking with the coach in several places—dark hallways, in her office, in a corner of the library. Always in private. He just assumed that they were having an affair. He confronted her. She denied it. He got furious and snapped. He just happened to be holding the pencil at the time. That's how it came to be the murder weapon."

They were all silent again. Murder was not the happiest subject of conversation.

Danny broke the silence. "Have you heard what they're going to do about a new football coach? I heard that the whole football team has been suspended from the college league for the rest of the year."

"I heard that, too," Crystal added. "That should give the Athletic Department time to hire a new coach. And, they have to."

Jade joined in the conversation, "I bet the next person they hire will have to answer a whole lot of questions about grades and sports and cheating. I don't envy anyone who steps into that job."

"Right," Danny said, "And we probably won't win many football games. At least for a while. What's going to happen to Coach Kelly?"

Crystal answered, "He was fired, of course, and his career is ruined. He won't be able to get a coaching job anywhere now. He's probably old enough that he could just retire. Or, maybe he has to change careers."

Danny and Jade nodded their heads.

Crystal continued, "Then there's Amber. Jade, girl, I don't think you need to worry about her anymore." Danny's face turned red at the mention of Amber's name.

Jade looked straight at him and he got even more uncomfortable.

"All right. All right," Danny said. "It was a mistake. But, hey, she was really the first clue to solving the case." He paused a second and looked at Jade before continuing, "And, God, how I wish I could have seen you take her down. The janitor said it was really something. He has a new respect for you."

This time Jade turned red.

Danny continued, "Anyway, she's been expelled from school. If she ever wants to come back, she'll have to wait at least a year then file a petition. By that time, we should all be at the Police Academy."

"Tiffany's gone, too," Crystal said. "She's going to be operating her business somewhere else."

Crystal turned her head back and forth from Jade to Danny. Then she pointed to the package on the table. "Danny. Let me see that thing again."

He picked up the package and unwrapped it. He smiled as he held up his plaque for everyone to see. It was wood with a metal plate attached to the front. There were letters printed on the metal. "For exceptional bravery in the duty of law enforcement, Danny Soto." The date was just below his name.

"Was it worth it?" Crystal asked.

Danny nodded. "I think so. Even though I've been assigned to parking ticket duty for the next three months."

"Hey," Jade said, "at least you get to write the tickets! I have to count them!"

Danny and Crystal laughed at this. "By the way, where is your plaque?" Danny asked her.

She raised one eyebrow and looked at him. "I don't have to carry it around with me to remember that I have it. I hung it in the den."

She looked directly at Danny now and spoke again, "And, I have to tell you. My mother thinks you are some kind of hero. She even wants to meet you."

Danny's mouth fell open. He closed it quickly. "Are you serious?" he asked.

Her eyes sparkled. "Yes," she said, "How about dinner some night this week with my mother and me?"

In response, Danny jumped up from his chair, pulled her to her feet and hugged her. He lifted her off the floor and danced around the small space near the table.

Crystal smiled and stood up. "I've got to go. I have some real police work to do." And she walked out the cafeteria doors.